THE CONSOLATION OF MAPS

Thomas Bourke was born in Ireland and lives in Italy. A graduate of University College Dublin, he is author of a book on relations between Europe and Japan. *The Consolation of Maps* is his first novel.

THE
CONSOLATION
OF
MAPS

Thomas Bourke

riverrun

First published in Great Britain in 2018 by riverrun

riverrun

An imprint of

Quercus Editions Limited
Carmelite House
50 Victoria Embankment
London EC4Y 0DZ

An Hachette UK company

Hardback 978 1 78648 759 9
Trade Paperback 978 1 78648 758 2
Ebook 978 178648 757 5

10 9 8 7 6 5 4 3 2 1

Typeset by CC Book Production
Printed and bound in Great Britain by Clays Ltd, St Ives plc

To my teachers

Francis O'Leary
Fr Henry Carroll OFM
Paddy Wynne

I

THE LIGHTS OF TOKYO made a celestial imprint on the ceiling of thick cloud. Kenji took the earthen path along the river and a shortcut through the alleys of Kawaguchi. Sparks showered across the floors of corrugated foundries near the station. It was not yet dawn on the last Thursday of November when the blue Keihin-Tohoku train arrived downtown. He let the icy wind blow open his overcoat as he approached the fish market near the Ginza. The auctions would be ending and he could have breakfast with the fishmongers and the last of the revellers.

As he approached the gallery Kenji's anxiety was heightened by the giant vertical banner with the title of the exhibition: *Artworks on Paper and Vellum*. This was the first time he'd seen the dark green canvas with gold leaf script. The gallery was on the seventh floor of a pre-war department store – one of the most exclusive in Tokyo. As a specialist in rare maps, Kenji's selection would share the exhibition hall with modern American prints and Italian architectural drawings. His chosen theme was 'Progress in Cartography'. Kenji followed the security guard inside. A light-box transparency of a fourteenth-century map flickered in the silent space. In the carpeted bays he nervously scanned his captions, rich in detail and conjecture. He tried to imagine what kind of impression the exhibition would make on someone seeing it for the first time. The maps were arranged to show the steady accumulation of knowledge towards accurate representations of Japan and the world. Exhibitions like this were located at the top of the building to entice visitors to the higher floors. Emporium exhibition openings were invitation-only Tokyo society events – attracting business executives, museum curators, celebrities and rival dealers. The prestige and purchasing power of the galleries made them the premier art dealerships in the city.

That evening a hundred purple irises were arrayed in the centre of the gallery under an art deco chandelier. Near the doorway a leather-bound visitors' book was bathed in soft light. Kenji nervously checked his business cards. But he didn't fidget with them – he'd been reprimanded for this as a junior. Be courteous without being condescending, they taught him. Carefully adjust your tone without compromising your authority. Engage the collector and the novice. Keep a certain distance. As the first patrons arrived Kenji unlocked the antique desk drawer and checked the list again. Although he didn't expect price enquiries during the reception, he memorised them in case someone asked.

Kenji was autonomous in his dealings – his superiors were less interested in rare maps than the lucrative market for modern art. Although he was the youngest of the departmental specialists, his colleagues thought his subject inaccessible and archaic. This gave him more freedom than his peers. When the gallery director passed through the gallery he wished Kenji well, but he didn't stop to view the maps. Nor did he notice the captions about a nineteenth-century astronomer to the Shogun, called Johannes Globius. This was the flourish in Kenji's homage to progress and a reminder of its price. It was only when the American arrived that Kenji found himself – for the first time in any language – sharing his embedded story. The fair-haired visitor was about thirty-five. He held the exhibition booklet open at Kenji's bilingual notes on the scientific importance and aesthetic beauty of antiquarian maps. Behind him was a Japanese woman in a buttoned overcoat who must have been an interpreter.

'This is a beautiful space,' said the man.

'It is,' said Kenji. 'Thank you.'

'All these old maps in such a modern gallery.'

'Past and present.'

'Precisely!'

The interpreter moved away when she heard them speaking English.

'I like this Martini map,' said the visitor.

'It is very fine,' said Kenji. 'The first we have ever had.'

'How's business?'

'Good. We are hoping 1989 will be even better.'

After the tension of imagined reactions, Kenji was relieved to speak freely. And he was pleased that the first person he was speaking to was a foreigner. Potential buyers and colleagues would take note. He explained to his guest that early European information about Asia was based on Marco Polo's speculations. Kenji showed him a 1522 woodcut with the insular Zinpangri – Japan – lying far off shore. The map was by Canon Martin Waldseemüller, the German cartographer who was first to use the word 'America' on a map. By associating the map in his exhibition with that historic work, Kenji was underlining the rarity and investment potential of his stock.

'How long have you worked in this place?' asked the American.

'Since leaving university,' Kenji replied. 'Four years.'

'You studied history – or geography?'

'I studied English literature – at Waseda University. I learned about maps when I started working here.'

'It's strange to see all this – in a department store, I mean.'

'I believe it was an American idea,' said Kenji in a well-rehearsed way. 'In the early days of our company, employees were sent to Wanamaker's for training.' He carefully pronounced their catchphrase. 'Best Philadelphia Tradition.'

'Wonderful!' said the visitor with a broad smile.

But when Kenji mentioned the demise of Altman's

department store in New York – and the on-site auction of maps, autographs, antiquarian books and paintings two years previously – the visitor was unsure if his host was speaking with regret or competitive satisfaction.

'The department stores of Japan have also changed,' Kenji added quickly. 'Many years ago – long before I came – there was a garden on the roof. There were telescopes and a small zoo.'

'A zoo?' the American repeated. 'Up there?'

'Yes. On the roof.'

'Great for clients.'

'It's our hope to put a telescope up there again,' said Kenji. 'I proposed this to our director. Visitors will compare the night sky with our celestial globes.'

He looked directly at his visitor. His face was pale. Perhaps he came straight from the airport, Kenji wondered.

'Are you in the art business, sir?'

'Yes – in New York. I'm Curtis Hahn.'

'Kenji Tanabe.'

As they exchanged cards a hostess approached with glasses of white wine on a silver tray.

'From Veneto in Italy,' said Kenji. 'Some of the architectural plans are by Palladio.'

'Thank you. Aren't you going to—'

'It is not allowed. Please – I want to show you something. It's the first Japanese map with parallels and meridians.'

The 1779 Revised Map of Japan and its Highways was

mounted in a simple lacquered frame. Kenji didn't say its author, Nagakubo Sekisui, came from his home town near the Pacific coast. Beside it were two subsequent iterations of the map showing progress towards a true outline of Japan. As Kenji spoke he felt his visitor was considering – for the very first time – the notion of rare Japanese maps. From the thousands of catalogues he'd seen, Kenji knew American galleries dealt mostly in western cartography. He silently rehearsed the prices again, prepared for the question. But the man didn't ask. He was there for something else. Then they moved to the final alcove – Kenji's favourite part.

'Every schoolchild knows about Tadataka Ino,' he said. 'He spent sixteen years surveying Japan. The drafting of the maps was not completed until 1821 – three years after he died. The Shogun didn't announce his death until the maps were ready. Tadataka Ino was a great man.' The posthumous map production, Kenji explained, was carried out by state cartographers under the Shogun's astronomer, Takahashi Kageyasu. His Latinised name was Johannes Globius. 'No trade version of that great work was issued until 1866. This is one of them. We can say ours is a first trade edition.'

In 1826, Globius met Philipp Franz von Siebold, a Bavarian scientist in the Dutch colonial service. Kenji explained that, although he knew that sharing maps with foreigners was a capital offence, Globius exchanged a copy of the new survey for books on exploration and maps of the Dutch East Indies. The ship on which von Siebold was to sail for Europe was damaged by a typhoon in Nagasaki Bay. The cargo was saved but officials discovered the maps. Von Siebold was deported. Globius was charged with treason.

Kenji noticed two clients waiting for him beside the guest book. He recognised them as curators from the Kobe City Museum, home to one of the finest collections in the country. He pretended not to notice.

'Four months after his arrest, the Shogun's astronomer died in prison. His body was preserved and the trial continued. He was found guilty of treason. The body was decapitated.'

The American paused, glanced at the two men and then spoke in a low, earnest voice. 'Would you be interested in working in America for a while? Kind of like those people who went to Wanamaker's.'

Although Kenji had no difficulty with his visitor's accent, he thought he'd misunderstood. The interpreter watched from behind the purple flowers.

'It's a business proposition – an opportunity,' the American added. Kenji bowed silently, then turned towards the men from Kobe.

The morning after the gala opening Kenji was startled to see the gallery director standing in the final alcove. He only visited the main gallery when important clients were expected.

'This is not right,' said the director in the tight air of

the silent space. His tone was simultaneously accusatorial and wounded. Kenji felt a cold sensation in his right ear, as though a draught had entered or gone out of his head. He had experienced this once before when, as a child, he overheard his mother asking the school doctor about autism.

'What's this?' the director asked, pointing towards the final exhibits.

'This is the—'

The director cut him off as he moved between the maps.

'There's been a complaint. The story of Tadataka Ino is not told the right way.'

'I don't understand,' said Kenji.

'He's a national hero. Why is there so much about this – this Globius? And scandal about a treason trial? There should be none of this!'

The security guard looked away, the keys tinkling on the ring in his white-gloved hand.

'It's the context, sir. Mapmaking in scientific and historical context. Globius was the Shogun's astronomer. He supervised the drafting of Tadataka Ino's charts. He made an important contribution to progress in mapmaking – in science.'

As he spoke, Kenji realised the director was reading the captions for the first time.

'Change it!'

The guard followed him out of the gallery. Kenji sat down at the bare, polished desk. After a few moments he got up and went to the visitors' book. He turned the pages, trying to guess who had complained. Perhaps a rival dealer, perhaps someone he'd refused a discount, perhaps a political man. He was sickened by the thought of having to rearrange the meticulously assembled narrative. He would be humiliated before his colleagues.

On the Saturday after the opening Kenji took the limited express to Mito, his home town seventy minutes north-east of Tokyo. At the railway station he spoke to the cobbler kneeling on the ground, his kit spread on a worn blue sack. The man, a friend of Kenji's father, asked him about the city. Kenji didn't say something had changed. He went to the Kairaku-en gardens where gnarled plum trees stood in ranks and tall bamboo swayed over darkened paths. He paused at the white rock fountain. His mother told him to bathe his eyes here when he started wearing glasses because the spring had curative properties. The nearby samurai lodge – a tourist attraction in summer – was deserted. He hadn't been inside since school but felt an urge to see it now. The rooms were decorated in homage to the plants outside: plum, peach, bamboo, maple, bush clover, cherry and chrysanthemum. The precise paintings were embellished with red blossoms, pale green leaves, ducks, parrots and a golden sun. Kenji stood for a moment at the entrance to the Room of Purity, white and empty. From an upstairs window he saw the gardens stretch out towards the sunless gleam of Lake Senba. Near the orchard gate, a woman in a heavy apron stoked a pyre of wood, scattering sparks high into the fading November light.

In the morning Kenji heard the shutter of his parents' bicycle shop that woke him each day as a boy. In the rain he walked to the construction site of the new Mito art complex. He smoked one cigarette after another as he gazed up at the strange molecular tower. At the glass doors workers tried to clear an untested drain. He watched them struggle, shoeless, poking the water as though trying to catch something. In the rain he walked to the central post office and phoned New York. When he introduced himself, the woman who answered seemed to sense his purpose. She ignored his request to speak to Mr Hahn and asked about his degree in English literature and the department store galleries of Tokyo. She interrupted him twice to take other calls. After a question about his exhibition she said it would be best if he came to America for interview. His fare would be paid on arrival. When she asked if he had any questions he said he had none.

11

KENJI STOOD IN THE freezing wind at Kennedy airport. The words *Happy New Year 1989 from Pan Am* were stencilled in blue on the glass doors. He touched the American business card in his overcoat pocket, wondering if anybody would come. Maybe it was all a misunderstanding or even some deception. More than an hour passed before a maroon Transit van slowed in front of the terminal. The window was rolled down and he heard his name. The driver was about his own age, wearing a woollen hat and a heavy jacket zipped to the chin.

'Mr Tanabe?'

'Yes, thank you.'

'My colleagues were hoping to meet you in New York. But something came up. We're going to headquarters – just outside Washington.'

When the driver began to smoke, Kenji put the creased business card in his pocket and took out the last of his Japanese cigarettes. In a tunnel that was longer and older than the tunnels of Tokyo he caught his reflection in America. At that moment he became fully aware of his decision. It was a decision met with silence in Tokyo. The director's stare didn't conceal his surprise. He seemed more preoccupied about finding and training a replacement for the map department than regretful about Kenji's departure. At the end of the year, when it was officially announced that Kenji would be leaving for America, the director made a brief speech and colleagues toasted him with wine left over from the exhibition opening.

When Kenji woke, the ground beside the Capital Beltway was covered in snow. They took the exit for Alexandria, continued along narrow suburban roads and came to a stop outside a red brick bungalow. The driver handed Kenji a single key.

'This is the guest house. Staff and trainees sometimes stay here. You can take any room – there's nobody else here now. I'll be back at nine.'

The door opened into a sparsely furnished parlour with a high glass atrium on one side. Kenji sat on the edge of a soft sofa, colourless in the dim light. The old cloth felt warm in the cold room. He closed his eyes, the hum of the engine still in his ears. Then he lay down and, fully clothed, drifted to sleep. Sometime in the night he dreamt that a telephone was ringing. Or maybe the ringing broke into his dream. In the morning the driver arrived on time. It was a ten-minute drive to the heavy open gates and the sloping driveway flanked with cypress trees. The words *Rare View* were engraved in green copper beside the door of a classic revival mansion. The driver took a fistful of Amoco gasoline receipts from his jacket and went into one of the offices. To Kenji the interior looked vast, stately and very old. At the end of an arched passageway there were rows of print chests in the middle of a library. Behind half-open doors there was the silence of a day yet to begin.

'Welcome to America.'

It was a woman's voice from the curved stairway. This was her second sentence. Startled, Kenji missed her first words. The voice had no music – but it was precise, even and captivating.

'How was your journey?'

'It was fine. Thank you.'

Her auburn hair swayed gently as she walked ahead of him into her office. Kenji guessed she was about forty-five. She wore a formal black jacket, a beige cardigan and black slacks.

'You're at the guest house?'

'Yes, it is very comfortable. Thank you.'

She shook her head. 'It's freezing. I know that for a fact. Get them to show you how to use the heating.'

Her office retained the homely warmth of the living room it had once been. A lavender carpet lay diagonally across the parquet floor. There was a fireplace with dried flowers, high bookcases and a large terrestrial globe in a wooden brace.

They stood facing each other across the long mahogany desk. She picked up an invoice from the neat stack of mail. There was no jewellery but Kenji noticed a large watch on her left wrist.

'Is this your first time in America?'

'Yes, the first time.'

'How old are you?'

'I'm twenty-six now.'

She gestured to an unframed map. 'It's the labyrinth at Versailles. Coronelli's globes were packed up there for a long time in the dust. Did you have a Coronelli in Tokyo?'

'Yes,' said Kenji. 'Not a globe – the map of Japan.'

'Curtis said great things about your exhibition. And that roof garden sounds wonderful. You gave him ideas for New York.'

'It's not there anymore – but we have photographs of how it looked a long time ago.'

'Did you have any American maps in the exhibition?'

'No.'

The flatness of this word made her look up from the invoice in her hand. Around her inquisitive eyes he noticed a darkness that could have been mascara or could have been permanent. She flicked open the Tokyo exhibition booklet. The sight of his own text made Kenji relax. For no reason he wondered if she smoked. She looked at his booklet again, then glanced at his bespectacled face.

'I like the way you mention Waldseemüller in this. The Library of Congress has been trying to get his great map for years. What kind of clients do you have in Japan?'

'We have businessmen, bankers, lawyers, museum curators—'

'Do you like them?'

'Yes,' Kenji said cautiously.

'Really?' She paced towards the high French doors. 'After so many years I'm beginning to prefer the stock.'

Kenji wondered why his résumé was not on her desk.

'What do you know about our company?'

'The catalogues. We've been receiving your catalogues for many years.'

He had studied these closely before the telephone conversation.

'Anything else?'

'Just the catalogues.'

'We have the best antiquarian stock in America. But we need to do more with Japan – more business – maybe open an office. Is that the sort of thing you could do?'

'Yes. I have four years' experience—'

'I've been to Tokyo. It was a sort of anniversary. We went to the theatre, the—'

'Kabuki.'

'Kabuki. It was beautiful. Do you like Kabuki?'

'Yes, our gallery is near the main theatre.'

She looked down at the invoice.

'When a boom is about to end the price of art goes up. Would you say it's like that?'

He hesitated.

'The market has been strong. I do not know what will—'

'The cycle is turning,' she said. 'We need to move quickly.'

This hung for a moment in the space between them. The word 'we' was strange – perhaps a signal. Later he thought this was the moment she made the decision to hire him. But one day he'd know that the decision had already been taken and that it wasn't an interview at all.

'Is there anything we should know about?'

'Excuse me?'

He was ready for this – the question about why he wanted to move. He had prepared an explanation while gazing up at the titanium art tower in Mito. He needed international experience. He needed to learn more about western maps and western business. But the woman standing on the other side of the desk meant something else. Maybe she sensed he was about to confess, because she quickly continued.

'Stock – maps we should buy.'

'I'll have to go through the catalogues.'

'If you think of any – write them down. And we need to know the reserve.'

'Reserve?'

'The lowest they'll accept,' she said impatiently. 'Don't worry – we won't send you.'

He knew by now that this was the woman he'd spoken to on the phone. She was at her New York gallery when he called from Japan.

'The job pays two thousand a month – plus four per cent commission on sales. That can be a lot. And accommodation at the guest house is free. We're a small company – so everyone helps with moving the stock – physical work. You don't mind?'

'No. We do that in Tokyo.'

He was about to ask about a work visa when a woman's voice crackled on the intercom.

'There's a call from Italy.'

She paused, then leaned towards the device. 'I'll take it upstairs.'

In the stinging silence after she left Kenji had time to take in the room. A perforated client list, red-lined with crayon, lay on the floor beside a stack of business magazines. A silk Dunhill foulard decorated with a London tramway map was draped on a chair. A clipping from the *Washington Post* was pinned to the bookcase. The date was 11 October 1965 and the headline read 'America of Vikings Shown on Pre-Columbian Map'. But Kenji couldn't read the salutation written in thick letters with two exclamation marks. In a Flemish exhibition poster a small monkey watched two men pondering a navigational task. A simple eighteenth-century plan of Alexandria hung over the fireplace. Near the desk there was a faded photograph of a map of Italy in a gilded frame. Kenji leaned in, realising that the map was neither a print nor a watercoloured chart – but a vivid fresco with the Mediterranean in aquamarine, mountains in earthen brown and plains in green. Through the window, at the end of the lawn of snow, Kenji was surprised to see a single Japanese Momiji tree. One day he would contrast the stillness of that room with what must have been the turmoil of her thoughts. Twenty minutes passed before he realised the interview was over and – unless it had been the first sentence he'd missed – she hadn't told him her name.

III

THEODORA APPEL DESCRIBED Rare View as a renaissance palazzo. There was no distinction between work and home – visitors were welcome day and night. A folding partition separated her office from the original dining room, now a reception area with antique desks and a row of metallic filing cabinets. It was here on the day after his interview that Kenji met the company secretary, a Dutch woman named Klara.

'Thea went to New York last night. She asked me to give you the news. You got the job.'

For an instant, Kenji felt something like alarm, then smiled and said, 'Thank you.'

'You can work here when you're not in the library,' said Klara, nodding towards the bare table opposite her desk. From this Kenji understood it would be best for him to work in the library.

'Come on, I'll show you around.'

Klara, the longest-serving employee, was hired from an

auction house in Amsterdam. She seemed a few years older than Appel and moved her short, slim body in an almost balletic way. Kenji followed her into the main gallery on the other side of the hallway. It was furnished in French imperial style with a large landscape oil painting to offset the delicate outlines of the maps.

'Our business is in the art market – but our roots are in the antiquarian book business,' she said, making this information sound official. Kenji followed her into the library where thousands of catalogues, reference works and journals were shelved in deep stacks between high windows. He instantly liked this space with its billiard-room lighting and familiar map chests – each with nine drawers. He quickly calculated that the library alone had twice as many maps as the Tokyo gallery.

'Our accounts department and Thea's apartment are upstairs,' said Klara. 'Did she tell you she started as a junior analyst on Wall Street?'

'No – there was a phone call while we were speaking.'

'Thea didn't like finance. She resigned after six months. She needs something real. That's what she always says about business – she needs something real. The brokerage had a corporate map collection. She loved that. When she was leaving they arranged a loan. She thought maps were undervalued and went to Europe to learn more. That's how I met her. I turned down her first offer – but she came back the next year.'

Klara explained how Theodora Appel reoriented the rare map business towards the more lucrative art business. Her success was a surprise to rivals and a source of resentment. Klara pulled a worn, ten-year-old magazine profile of Appel from a drawer.

'*Theodora Appel is an innovative businesswoman with a determined approach,*' she read, adding for Kenji's benefit, 'That's what's called a euphemism in English. Some dealers found her too sharp.' She continued: '*Theodora Appel has raised the stakes in what used to be a conservative trade. Her reputation has grown quickly because of her constant and confident reinvestment in high calibre stock. Proof of this is the well-stocked and quickly expanding collection of rare maps in the carefully arrayed print chests at her gallery home in Alexandria. But a recent visitor to the mansion was surprised to find most of the other rooms completely empty.*'

Klara told Kenji that Appel first worked from the house in Alexandria she bought on her thirtieth birthday and renamed Rare View. Three years later she rented a gallery on 57th Street in Manhattan. By then she had ceased to consider map and book dealers as competitors. Two years later she bought the premises. Klara gave him the magazine and he read the article closely – paying particular attention to the carefully composed photograph of Appel. It was not the portrait he expected, because there were no maps. The picture showed Appel standing in overgrown grass with Rare View behind her. She wore a white cotton dress with the arms of a suede jacket tied at her neck. Her left hand brushed the auburn hair from her face as she smiled at the camera. A white dog, which Kenji only noticed the second time he read the article, was galloping between the cypress trees in the distance.

'We're art dealers,' Appel said to Kenji on one of her sudden visits to the library. 'We're in competition with auctioneers, stockbrokers, yacht salesmen. Our business is about rarity, service and confidentiality.'

Kenji knew such observations were part of his instruction and wrote them in a gilt-edged notebook as Appel moved impatiently from drawer to drawer. This knowledge would be valuable when he returned to Japan as Appel's sales agent in Tokyo.

'Hundreds of millions of dollars are being spent on modern art,' she continued.

'It is very popular in Japan – we had five specialists at the gallery.'

'Lobbyists and doctors can't afford it. Here we give them the opportunity to acquire something else – high-quality historical artefacts. There are thirty thousand potential clients in Washington – and more than three times that number in New York – who can spend at least a hundred thousand a year on art.'

Kenji presumed the source of these statistics was

somewhere in the stack of business magazines he'd seen in her office.

'The difference between the two cities is Buyer's Remorse. Unfortunately it's now recognised in law. They have a few days to reverse the sale. It happens in Washington – it's rare in New York.'

Appel's business advice contrasted with her loving narratives about the maps. Klara mentioned this during Kenji's orientation. 'Thea's knowledge of cartography is encyclopaedic – she hypnotises clients. The maps are her reservoir. Especially since—'

It was only now, as Kenji observed Appel across the polished tops of the map chests, that he recalled this sudden halt of Klara's and wondered why she had changed the subject. For an instant it distracted him from Appel's explanation of how mapmaking relied on astronomy and navigation, the dead reckoning of Phoenician sailors, the guarded secrets of court astronomers and the manoeuvring of admirals and generals. The sixteenth century was a precarious time for cartographers, who had to weigh the conflicting accounts of sailors, merchants and missionaries. The growth of commerce and the expansion of maritime networks led to the rise of a more scientific cartography. Portuguese, Spanish and Italian manuscript charts showed coastlines with greater accuracy. These gold-embellished manuscripts commanded the highest prices. Appel had a passionate, physical understanding of them. In Japan the maps were rarely touched.

Kenji had been trained to make formal presentations – often rehearsed under the impatient eye of the director – ending with a formal statement of provenance. But during Appel's tutorials the tops of the walnut chests were strewn with maps. She gripped Kenji's arm and pulled him close to show how copperplate engravings left minute traces where the soft metal had been retooled for new discoveries. In her office she spent hours leaning over newly acquired maps, noting microscopic differences in condition, impression and pigment.

'Even printed maps are unique,' she told him. 'No strike is exactly the same. Hand-colouring is never identical. And don't ever use the word "obsolete" with a client. Nothing this beautiful can ever be obsolete. That's why we never lower our prices. We can offer some clients a ten per cent discount – but this is already priced in from the start.'

Appel told Kenji she sometimes recognised the very map she'd sold years before at an antiques show in Connecticut or Chicago. Her meticulous catalogue descriptions began as a sketch – a map of a map – on a canary legal pad with marginalia about obsolete names, coats of arms and Latin legends.

'Each detail is a potential hook for clients – an opportunity to justify our prices,' she told him. These notes were also the foundation of her finely printed catalogues which flaunted the technical mastery she used to impress clients: ground eggshell in renaissance ink, gum arabic to stabilise colouring, woodcuts on mulberry paper and silk rebacking by her own restorer in Washington. 'You'll have to meet him,' she said. 'The man's a genius.'

In his notebook Kenji transcribed the unfamiliar terms she used, like 'cockling' – the small waves in tanned sheepskin called vellum; and 'rhumb lines' – the sixteen compass directions in portolan charts. Her descriptions were admired even by the editor of the *Washington Post*, who sent a letter humorously regretting that he couldn't afford an eighteenth-century map of Chesapeake Bay. Although Appel's visits at first made Kenji nervous, now he gently turned the cigarette pack in his pocket. This was his habit while listening to his favourite literature professor in Tokyo. Or while talking to the girl from the ceramics department whose sparkling lips made him smile, but whom he couldn't hear above the roar of the night train back to his tiny apartment in Kawaguchi.

Each morning Appel distributed invoices, letters and catalogues to the dozen staff gathered around her desk. These meetings were interrupted by phone calls conducted with an openness that astonished Kenji, who was trained in the formal Tokyo art world. 'Do you like what you do?' Appel asked a museum curator she was trying to hire for the New York gallery. On another occasion Kenji heard her use the same question as an invitation to resign. He took Appel's method to be the American way of business – not realising that other dealers treated her as an outsider. During the staff meetings maps in acid-free cards with mylar protection were pencilled with purchase codes and divided between Rare View and New York. Newly framed maps leaned against the walls. Maps on consignment were stacked in antique racks. Maps were on hold for favoured clients. Maps were on loan to exhibitions – inclusion in a catalogue could double their price. Appel feared the stock would be seen as stale, so hundreds of maps were rotated between Rare View and New York. The company interns – many of them related to Appel's society clients – sat on the carpet in her office to see the watermarks and traces of Frankfurt ink in the maps she held up to the light. Kenji joined them, sitting in awkward western style as she explained the importance of condition, original colouring – and a selling technique she called 'proposing'. Kenji had seen this when a woman from Chicago came to buy a map for her husband. Appel had prepared a selection of maps before the appointment, and began by telling a story about each one. But her narrative was more than a story, it was almost an invitation to share some common memory – even if this memory were only a suggestion. Her quick but gentle tone became more conversational with every observation made by the client. And then she made the proposal: 'Shall we discard these two?' Sometimes the proposal was more direct – but it always contained the word 'we' which Appel also used in her proposal to Kenji on the day of his interview. When choices were narrowed she manoeuvred one of the maps into the hands of the client – sometimes by asking them to hold it up to the light while she pointed to the watermark or an outline of verdigris.

In the library Kenji kept his notebook, a magnifying loupe and a flask of vintage sake he had intended to give his new employer before the phone call from Italy took her from the room. That moment had passed. It didn't seem appropriate to give it to her now. He spent hours each day updating the mailing list. 'In a viable business,' Appel told him, 'this task is never done.' She was skilled at maintaining contacts over time. When a client stopped buying she offered to buy back maps she'd sold years before. So successful was her remaking of the rare map business that the retail price of the past could be the wholesale price of the present. Staff made calls about the regular replacement of acrylic glass – necessary for the protection of framed maps. Every contact provided an opportunity to sell or to buy. Appel bought from lawyers and executors, she bought at auction and she bought from former staff whose businesses had failed. She offered discreet tax and insurance advice to clients. In quiet moments she browsed old sales records and asked Kenji to phone clients at random. He was her research assistant, he accompanied her on appointments, and he delivered maps and atlases to clients in Washington, Virginia and Delaware even though his international driving licence was only for tourist use. Appel asked him to translate the company brochure into Japanese and encouraged him to make whatever changes were appropriate. Many of her phrases were diffi-cult, or impossible, to render. But this exercise slowly helped him find a voice that was fresh, erudite and free. While he believed that Appel valued his ability to help her access the Japanese art market, he also understood that his very presence – as a new and unfamiliar listener – was somehow of even greater value to her.

Outside the Library of Congress in the last week of Jan-uary, Kenji stared into the frozen basin of the Neptune fountain. While waiting for his reader's card he thought about his ninety-day visa. He wondered how long it would take for Appel to decide about an office in Japan. What would happen if he overstayed? He walked along the great avenues lined with cherry trees, Lebanese cedar and Asian magnolia. At the Corcoran Gallery he stood before American landscapes by artists with unfamiliar names. At the National Archives he studied a land-claim map by an Ioway Indian chief. At the National Gallery he examined a portrait, tentatively identified as Ptolemy, holding an astrolabe and wearing a strange silken headscarf. What-ever Ptolemy might have looked like, Kenji was sure he never looked like this. He watched limousines with blue, white and red diplomatic plates arriving at the Monocle restaurant. He imagined decisions of importance being taken there. These were Appel's clients. He walked for miles along the tide waters, like he used to walk along the Arakawa on his way to the train station. At Arlington he found the tomb of Major L'Enfant who drafted the original plan of Washington. A relief map was engraved in the marble. Across the Potomac the posthumous city was spread out in white.

'What have you been doing?' Appel asked as he passed her door. It was a question she frequently threw out at meetings – sometimes as a reprimand. More often it was an impatient invitation to come up with something new. At first this was alien to Kenji because the director of the Tokyo gallery never asked for suggestions. But Kenji had prepared for this moment by rehearsing a proposal at the guest house.

'I've been thinking that some of the maps could be shown in a public space – maybe a corporate foyer or a department store.'

'Yes?'

'I found an old booklet in the library. It was published by the American Geographical Society in 1913. They made stained-glass copies of famous maps and put them in the windows of a lecture hall. We could borrow some of them to exhibit beside our maps.'

He repeated the department store strategy that so fascinated Curtis Hahn at the exhibition in Tokyo. Appel patiently waited for him to finish. Then he realised why. There was a man standing motionless in the hallway beyond the open door.

'Come on in, Scott. Meet our newest recruit! This is Kenji – from Japan.'

'Pleased to meet you,' said the man, clearing his throat.

'It is a pleasure,' said Kenji.

He was about sixty, wearing a gabardine overcoat and carrying a leather portfolio of maps for sale. Appel didn't seem surprised by his arrival but the man seemed nervous – as though he'd been summoned.

'Scott used to work for us,' she said. 'Now he has a business of his own.'

'Well, it's—'

'He's one of our graduates – so to speak. We still work together – even though he's the competition now.'

She laughed lightly and Scott made a forced smile as he laid the maps on the desk. Kenji was surprised when he accepted her first offer. Most dealers and runners bargained with her – playfully, nervously or pleadingly. She picked up the phone and signalled him up to the accountant's office. His slow steps were heavy on the wooden stairs. Kenji studied the inset view of New York in the corner of the first map.

'He's coming up now,' Appel said into the receiver. 'Fifty thousand the lot. Use the New York account.'

She glanced at the map.

'Nieuw Amsterdam is a beautiful name.'

'Yes, it is,' said Kenji.

'I had it before,' she said.

'I once saw one at the—'

'That very map,' said Appel, carefully removing the cellophane wrapper from an art magazine. 'The next one as well.'

Kenji looked at the second map.

'This one as well?'

'All of them,' she said.

'How do you—'

'He stole them from me.'

There was a light, almost satisfied, tone in her voice – as though possession of this knowledge outweighed the loss.

'Four years ago.'

'Can't you—'

'Oh yes,' she said. 'But it takes years in the courts – we might even fail. Provenance among dealers is a very difficult business. And I need the stock now. Buying is as important as selling. The origin is as important as the final destination. Indeed, there is no final destination. It's an endless cycle. Through time. We merely try to add value – add appreciation. Besides, he's no businessman – you can see that, can't you?'

Kenji never answered questions like this.

'He was once a great salesman – one of the very best. He could match stock to clients perfectly. And he was charming.

But on his own . . .' Her voice trailed to a whisper as she looked down at the desk. 'These maps – these beautiful maps – the way they come back.'

The footsteps were on the stairs again. Each one was heavy with thought. His voice broke the stillness of the room.

'Thank you, Theodora.'

Kenji thought the man sensed what they'd said. Perhaps Appel did too because she quickly replied, 'A pleasure, Scott,' in the same bright tone that welcomed Kenji to America. 'Always keep us in mind.'

'I'll do that, Theodora,' he said, picking up the empty leather case.

'Come on, I'll walk you out.'

The door was opened. Freezing air rushed inside and swirled up the curved stairway. Kenji reluctantly heard their final words.

'Theodora,' he said. 'What happened? To Jack, I mean. I only found out—'

'A brain haemorrhage.'

Papers lifted in the draught. Kenji pressed them to the desk.

'The anniversary is soon.'

'I just wanted to say something.'

'I remember,' said Appel. 'He was your pal.'

*

In the evenings, when the staff went home, Kenji took off his shoes and silently paced the floorboards. Rare View was warmer than the guest house – Klara called it the 'ghost house'. In the library Kenji spent hours examining a rare English edition of the great Abraham Ortelius atlas. The date 1606 was tooled on the spine of the calf-bound map-book with the title *Theatrum Orbis Terrarum* – Theatre of the World. Its musky scent reminded Kenji of the mound of old newspapers in the corner of his father's bicycle shop. He once handled the Latin edition in Tokyo but had never seen the English text, which compared the volcanoes of Japan with Mount Etna in Sicily.

Kenji reclassified the library because he felt slow locating the information Appel needed from the gazetteers of place names and carto-bibliographies. He made separate sections for histories of geography, atlases of history and auction catalogues from Sotheby's and Christie's. Appel regularly asked him to check Sabin's *Bibliotheca Americana*, a twenty-nine-volume work that added a gravitas to American history Kenji hadn't anticipated. The deep shelving, stacked with limited edition facsimiles and folio atlases, absorbed every sound. When people spoke there was, to Kenji's ear, a pleasing distance in their voices. Appel's sudden requests for information were also invitations to watch her work.

One day in late January she said to him, 'I'm having trouble with a letter. It's almost a personal one. She's Italian

– about your age. She used to work here.' She didn't look up from the dossier on her desk. 'If you think of anything – impressions about this place—'

She must have sensed Kenji's confusion because she continued softly, 'She was a special employee. I'd like to get her back.'

Kenji thought Appel asked for this because the company had no personnel department. Appel made all recruitment decisions and staff files were managed by two accountants. Afterwards Kenji thought she might have asked him for suggestions because he too was a foreigner. He might have similar impressions of Rare View. He had seen the woman's name – Maria Manetti – and her diminutive initials in ledgers and price codes. It was her abandoned desk he used when he wasn't in the library. Klara said Maria was Appel's most valued confidante. 'Thea trusted her completely – and she needs Maria back here now. We got sued up in New York. That's exactly the kind of thing Maria would have resolved before it got out of hand. The New York director resigned six months ago. It was a fight about maps we were offered. Thea has a rule – all the galleries do – employees have to declare before buying maps on their own account. This includes anything they come across outside work. Thea has first refusal. If she declines, employees are free to trade.'

To Kenji this was bizarre. Japanese galleries forbade all personal trading. To encourage adherence to the rules, Klara explained, staff were paid commission on maps they found for the company. The New York director claimed he hadn't received a reply from Appel about a cache of colonial era maps. Appel countered that the maps were not properly attributed. The director was fired. Then he sued.

'It went on until last month,' said Klara. 'Thea settled the day before the first hearing. We lost a lot. Maria would have gone up there and done a deal. She'd have got him seven or eight per cent – well above the regular commission. Thea wouldn't even have asked for details – they had that kind of understanding. Without Maria there have been a lot of problems – especially between here and New York. Ross – the director who left – will probably open a gallery. He knows the right people. Thea's become too edgy – she's not interested in small talk and people pick it up the wrong way. She was more natural – more social – before. She's taking more risks – it's not like her. We need Maria back here.'

In the library Kenji read his draft of the letter. He had no idea what Appel wanted. When the phone rang late that evening, he had reduced the text to just four succinct sentences. Kenji was expecting the call from his literature professor in Tokyo. The professor would be coming to a conference in New York and needed some advice. Kenji wrote down the dates and told the professor about his new position. As he spoke from the faraway library, he realised how much he'd learned from Theodora Appel. Later Kenji thought he'd spoken too much – but his professor seemed to enjoy their conversation – he might even have been impressed. When he hung up, Kenji took a fresh sheet and quickly wrote down a new draft of the letter in Japanese. Then he made a precise translation and took it to Appel's office. The room was drained of colour but every object was sharply etched by the ethereal glow from the snow beyond the French doors. He could see his own pale reflection in the framed museum poster as he stepped forward to place the single paragraph in the centre of her desk.

IV

A T T H E E N D O F January Kenji saw New York in daylight for the first time. He was in the city for the Winter Antiques Show, the most important in America. 'It generates leads for half the year,' explained Klara as she unlocked the door of Appel's gallery in an art nouveau building on 57th Street. 'We're closed for the ten days of the show. Everyone's at the Park Avenue Armory setting up the booth.'

The gallery was more formal than Rare View, with ornate desks, rosewood chairs, Persian carpets and printed wallpaper instead of simple federal paint – all under the amber glow of a Venetian chandelier suspended from a gilded chain.

When they arrived at the Armory there were dozens of vehicles at the service entrance. Six of Appel's salesmen were unloading Bakelite print cases from Volvo estate cars. Among them was Curtis Hahn, who came to the opening of the Tokyo exhibition. He looked younger in a corduroy jacket, woollen hat and hiking boots.

'You took our offer!'

'Yes. Thank you, Mr Hahn.'

'Call me Curtis. You made a bold move, Kenji.'

'I must learn more.'

'Theodora likes you – that's what I hear. To be honest, here in New York we're relieved she's found someone like you.'

Kenji didn't know what this meant. For an instant the city was silent.

'What is your job in the company?'

Two of the salesmen glanced over as Curtis laughed into the winter wind.

'Everything! Buying, selling, shows like this – that trip to Japan. I've been to Italy since then. Anything's possible with this company. You know what I love most about Theodora? She gives everyone a chance. Everyone. And now there's been a shake-up – I'm deputy director! It's a strange company. Not a company at all. Don't you see that?'

The shouts of carpenters, electricians and porters rang through the vast army drill hall. Near the high service doors a security guard with a revolver checked the identities of all who entered. The aisles were streaked by the wheels of hand-trucks hauled through sidewalk slush. Seventy booths transformed the hall into a transient museum. Eighteenth-century salons with gilded mirrors rose beside galleries with old master pictures, tapestries, American painted furniture, antique jewellery, longcase clocks and classical statuary. Florida flowers cascaded from monumental vases along the aisles. Alcoves of leather-bound books gave a scent of permanence. The dealer beside Appel's booth offered a shock of George Washington's hair in a silver and glass case.

Kenji presumed that the gala opening, with the mayor, celebrity designers and philanthropists, would be a black tie event. He rented a tuxedo near the Whitney Museum and, an hour before the opening, took the wide gothic stairway up past the dealers' bar to the quiet trophy-lined corridor at the top of the building. As he adjusted his bow tie under the bronze bust of a general, he was startled to see two women in nightgowns smiling at him. A man wheeling a cylindrical coffee pot rang a bicycle bell. About thirty women came out of a long parquet dormitory with cots on either side. As Kenji moved among them he realised this was the women's shelter – one of the beneficiaries of the opening gala. When he descended to the great hall, the tuxedo drew smiles from the New York gallery staff. All wore business suits. Curtis, the only one he recognised, smiled encouragingly.

Appel was in the corner of the booth, facing a framed Dürer star map. She was dressed in one of the black two-piece suits she wore at Rare View. It was as though she were always ready. Here the simple elegance was exactly right. Her only concession to the New York occasion was a fine gold necklace with a single pearl. When Kenji heard her voice he realised she wasn't examining the framed map at all, but recording instructions about clients into a black dictaphone. 'Cancel that guy on 79th and Fifth – his wife is on the West Coast – it's her money . . . Send the architect a copy of Tooley's map dictionary – sign it from me . . . "Last chance syndrome" – the staff need to use this more . . . Get the caterers in for lunch at the gallery on Saturday. And this year it's for buyers only – no deadbeats.'

She turned swiftly and caught his gaze. He expected her to say something about the tuxedo. But she didn't notice, or pretended not to notice.

'If Mr Peters comes – bring him straight to me.'

'Mr—'

'Find me – and interrupt. You understand? It's important. Lewis Peters.'

Four salesmen were at minor tasks – one of them pacing back and forth along the boundary of the booth's ornate carpet, as though this were the limit of a cage. He was memorising the contents of a page in his hand.

'What time is that reception over?' Appel asked.

'The Benefactors? At nine,' said Curtis.

She glanced at her watch.

'We need to get started.'

'They're complaining about the heat.'

'Who?' she asked.

'The antique furniture dealers – problems with the wood or something.'

Appel looked along the aisle.

'I'm glad we're in maps. Paper and vellum – they're tough.' She tapped the mahogany bureau from the gallery. 'Remember what I said about the client list.'

'We can share leads now,' said Curtis.

'Only with dealers who do well here. Who sell.'

'Swap clients.'

'Yes,' she said tersely. 'Furniture dealers wouldn't think of that.'

She coached Kenji while the booth was quiet.

'Every object has a story. Put the map in their hands and tell that story. You saw how we did that with the lady from Chicago. And don't worry about questions. Don't waste time competing with their obsessions. Listen to their interests but don't let them take over. This is the most important antiquarian event in America. We have ten days to max-imise our return on this stock. Don't spend too much time with scholars – they know too much and they don't have money. And remember the rule – after forty minutes it's just a conversation – you need to close the sale or move on.'

The salesman with the piece of paper paced to and fro. Curtis peered into the distance like a rifleman. As she spoke to Kenji, Appel's voice seemed agitated but lost none of its clarity. 'We have ten days. Ten days to harvest and plant for the year – that's it. Ten days to sell. Most of the people who come to the Winter Show have been here before. They come back. They're on the boards of companies and museums – they're important people and they like fine things to impress their friends. They like to impress with money. So we have to impress with quality. Quality and relevance – that means matching the maps to their lives – to their stories. That's why we put the maps – the right maps – in their hands. If you make the right connection – the right proposal – you will create appreciation. For them, for us and for these objects.'

As she spoke, Kenji recalled the photograph in the magazine profile. Appel now looked more like this portrait, he thought. It was the light. The spotlights in the booth were warm – contrasting with the darkness high up in the barrel vault supported by wrought-iron beams. Maybe it was this blend of high darkness and museum-quality lighting that gave the drill hall the semblance of a series of stages – each presenting an ensemble from a moment in the past.

As the booth began to fill, Kenji watched Appel greet clients by name and enthusiastically share her new acquisitions. Maybe she enjoyed him watching her work – the other salesmen seemed distant or wary.

'He's with me,' she snapped at an interior decorator who was waiting for Kenji to step back from an exchange he thought confidential. The decorator wanted to broker a map with a client.

'It's the light,' he explained. 'We need to see it in the client's apartment.'

'You don't,' said Appel. 'We can do that any other time of the year. But not during the Winter Show. Bring the client here—'

'It's my client, Theodora.'

'Do you think I'd cut you out, Robert?' He didn't answer. 'Bring the client to the booth. We'll sell this – and more. I'll give you six. That's two points above my own people.'

Sometimes she drew strangers together, introduced them and launched an animated presentation that gradually became a proposal. These proposals were modulated for every visitor; soft and humorous with a couple from Connecticut, brisk with a woman who might have been scouting for a London gallery. For a banker from Morgan there was one declamatory sentence: 'This is for you.' This was proposing as closure. The beginning as end. The technique exhilarated Appel's most important clients – as though they were receiving a gift. Such people had first refusal on important new stock, and to emphasise this privilege the price was never negotiable. Such clients had absolute faith in her judgement. She slipped the banker's card under the protective mylar and locked the map in a drawer. When he left, Appel went back to the corner like a boxer and turned on the dictaphone. Kenji was observing her method when he saw his professor from Tokyo approach the booth. He once again became conscious of his tuxedo.

'Professor,' Appel asked when Kenji introduced them, 'was he a good student?'

'Yes. He has a wonderful memory. And he is a very good translator. I still ask for his advice.'

'He's doing a lot of translating for us. It has greatly helped us in the Japanese market.'

The professor, who was slightly shorter than Appel, wore a grey metallic suit – fashionable at that time in Tokyo. The colour matched his trimmed moustache, making him look younger than his sixty-five years.

'You have beautiful things here,' he said. 'Beautiful.'

'Do you collect, Professor?'

There was a flicker of incomprehension behind his smile before he said in a self-deprecating way: 'Just old postcards. They are a valuable record of old Tokyo – the parts that do not exist now.'

'Views,' said Appel. 'I collect them as well – mostly from Italy. My house is called Rare View.'

'Professor Kobayashi is here for a conference at Columbia University,' said Kenji. 'He translates Emily Dickinson into Japanese.'

'I love Emily Dickinson,' said Appel. And before Kenji had time to decide if this were sales talk, she surprised him.

'*Because I could not stop for Death – He kindly stopped for me.*'

When Kenji saw his professor's stunned expression he felt a surge of pride.

'It is one of the greatest poems. It is as though her poetry were made—'

There was the exaggerated flash of an official photographer and a small commotion in the aisle. Appel calmly turned to Kenji.

'I need you to meet her. She's the most famous Japanese artist in New York – in all of America, in fact. It'll just be a few words.'

Klara was escorting the woman, who was wearing sunglasses, towards Appel's booth in case other dealers cut in – a common problem at the fiercely competitive Winter Antiques Show. His professor was already backing away at the sight of their celebrity guest.

'Give your professor a private tour of the gallery tomorrow,' Appel said to Kenji. 'And take him to dinner at the Giardinetto – 75th and Third. Put it on my account.'

'Thank you, Miss Appel,' said the professor, waving back. 'It has been joyous to meet you.'

Appel presented Kenji to her most famous client, and they exchanged short pleasantries in Japanese as he handed her his new card. Then the three women moved ahead of the photographer towards the dealers' lounge. Kenji earnestly scanned the aisle to see if his professor were still nearby – he'd forgotten to give him his newly translated catalogue. But he'd disappeared in the gala throng.

Then he heard a man say, 'It's quite magnificent.'

He was looking up at the large bird's-eye view of Venice. Although not addressing anyone in particular – Kenji had been looking out of the booth – they were only a yard apart.

'It's by Jacopo de'Barbari,' said Kenji, still peering down the aisle for his professor. 'From the year 1500.'

'The detail is extraordinary – microcosmic.'

'It was printed from six pearwood panels,' said Kenji, word for word from Appel's catalogue.

'Where did you get it?'

The man's casual delivery did not conceal the bluntness of the question.

'From the collector we sold it to,' said Kenji, quoting the phrase Appel frequently used at Rare View. 'He sold it back to us.'

The man's sturdy shoulders stiffened in his tight jacket as he recognised the stock answer. He turned to Kenji. His brown hair was combed straight back from his tanned forehead.

'You're new, aren't you?'

'I work in Alexandria. My name is Kenji Tanabe.'

The man considered this for a moment.

'You must be Ms Manetti's replacement. Do you know Maria?'

'Maria?' Kenji hesitated. 'No, I do not.'

The visitor looked up at the great panorama of Venice. Kenji now realised who he was.

'They sold a statue over there – for a million. That's what I like about the Winter Show – it's got real class.'

'Would you like to join our mailing list, sir?'

The man deflected this invitation with a quick blink.

'When you see Theodora, tell her I'll come by later. It's Lewis Peters.'

After he'd left, Kenji asked Klara about the man.

'We met him at the Winter Show five years ago. He's a property developer. Thea asked Maria to look after the account. He bought some very big items. Then he went away – nothing for three years. Maria didn't like him, but she never said why. He called last week and said he'd be coming to this year's show. And Theodora wants to see him.'

Lewis Peters returned to the booth an hour later.

'Welcome back,' said Appel.

'Theodora!' he said with a slight gasp. 'Beautiful. The booth is beautiful.'

'It's a great show this year. And we have lots of new things – but there wasn't time to frame them. You have to come to Alexandria as soon as possible.'

In contrast to her insistence that she be told as soon as Peters arrived, Appel's demeanour was now more professional than warm. This impression was reinforced a few minutes later when – seeing the interior decorator return with a man she recognised – Appel abruptly cut away from Peters.

'You said it was a client, Robert.'

'This is—'

'I know who this is, Robert. This is a dealer.'

'He's a client of mine. A dealer-client – but a client.'

'He's a dealer. And that won't work, Robert. You have to tell me—'

'Theodora—'

'I don't need sales like this,' said Appel. 'This isn't whole-sale.'

The decorator saw his commission slipping away.

'But we agreed—'

'This is my show, Robert. You can go now.'

The others were perplexed, but Klara understood. She later told Kenji that this moment of bravado had little to do with the hapless decorator's behaviour.

'I think she was somehow showing off to Mr Peters,' said Klara to Kenji. 'She needs to impress people like that – to show she's in charge. He hasn't been around for a few years, and . . .' She paused as a thought came to her. 'I wonder if he's back because Jack isn't here. This is Theodora's first Winter Show without Jack Berman. She was devastated when he died.'

Klara and Curtis were the last to leave the booth on the opening night of the Winter Antiques Show. The high lamps were dimmed and the security guards were already pacing the aisles. There was a pleasant scent of fresh wax on the wooden floor. From the lounge there was a trembling tinkle of empty glasses.

'Did you speak to Kenji?' asked Klara.

'Yes – of course. Everything's fine.'

'Does he know it was Theodora?'

'That she ordered the complaint in Tokyo? No, he doesn't. We paid that interpreter very well.'

'He fits in. Theodora trusts those who don't talk.'

'Were you like that, Klara?'

'I suppose I was at first. I didn't know anyone. I didn't know what was going on.'

'What is going on?' asked Curtis.

'She's suddenly talking about a gallery in Tokyo – and about Florence.'

'Again?'

'Nothing's decided. Not yet. But she seems set on some kind of change – some risk.'

Near the great doors, four workmen carefully hoisted an imperial Roman torso from a wooden plinth. The sturdy breastplate exuded power. A handwritten *Sold* sign was attached to the base.

'It was a million,' said Curtis.

'How do you know?'

'Lewis Peters bought it.'

'He told you that?'

'No,' said Curtis. 'Kenji found out. He spoke to the dealer. People tell him things.'

For ten days Kenji shuttled maps between the 57th Street

gallery and the Park Avenue Armory. He quickly learned the rhythm of New York's alternate parking geography and how to navigate the ice in the narrow streets. He prepared a dossier of Californiana – a personalised catalogue – for a film producer Appel met at the Winter Show, and delivered it to the Plaza hotel. 'Never underestimate the value of special delivery in this business,' she told him. He included photographs of an uncoloured Briggs map of the Goodly Iland of California and a 1666 Dutch sea chart of t'Eylandt California by Pieter Goos – confidently showing California lying off the American coast. In his research note Kenji compared the California-as-island controversy with a similar debate among geographers in Japan. The Shogun's astronomer speculated about whether Sakhalin was a peninsula of Tartary or an island in the Pacific. Early European maps showed lower California as a peninsula. It was subsequently shown as an island – then as a peninsula again. Kenji didn't like such regressions in cartography – they contravened his faith in scientific progress. He wouldn't have acknowledged the California controversy except the chronology exposed it so clearly.

The Winter Antiques Show was taken down on a wet Monday morning. The rain brought relief from the cold but flooded the Lexington Avenue service entrance. As darkness fell the roads were icy again. On the turnpike Kenji thought of the homeless women – like angels – high above the party in nightgowns. He thought about Appel's stage-like performance in the booth. Here – at least for a while – she could forget the grief that was in her heart. In the vast temporary store of the past, someone was missing. Kenji hadn't considered Appel's past life until the day Scott, the map runner, had asked about Jack during his strange visit to sell maps back to Appel. What had she been like before the death of the man she must have loved? To Kenji she seemed complete the first day he'd seen her on the stairway at Rare View. Now he realised her life had changed – that she must have been different before – but he couldn't imagine how. Many times he returned to the profile in the magazine Klara had given him. And many times he studied Appel's face in the photograph standing in the overgrown grounds of Rare View – her hand in motion and even her eyes smiling, narrow against the sun.

As he approached Washington, Kenji missed the Beltway exit for Alexandria. He lit a cigarette, turned up the radio and circled the city again. It was after midnight when he arrived at Rare View. He picked up his mail in the ante-chamber and carried the Bakelite map cases into the library. There was a letter from his mother, a postcard from the girl with sparkling lips on the night train, and an envelope with his first month's pay in cash. He went back to the car and started the engine for the short drive to the guest house. There in the beams he was startled to see a young woman standing on the lawn staring up at the light in Theodora Appel's window.

V

MARIA MANETTI ALMOST DIDN'T make the phone call that left Kenji alone in Appel's office on the day of his interview. She was visiting a friend in Florence when she noticed the estate agent's sign on the palazzo in Via Santo Spirito, where Jack Berman had lived. When she met the agent the following afternoon he was surprised to see a woman not yet thirty, dressed in a long woollen coat. But he didn't take her less seriously than an older client. When Maria asked to see the uppermost apartment the agent explained that all floors were now vacant. The building was for sale as a single lot.

'The electricity is out,' he said, pulling a small flashlight from the pocket of his green overcoat. 'They're fixing it in a few days.'

For a moment he let the light play on Maria's pale complexion and long black hair. From her accent, he guessed she was from Lombardy and she said he was right. She followed his disoriented shadow up the serene grey steps. The sturdy door at the top of the palazzo was ajar. The agent pressed it slowly. Low January rays shone through the terrace fanlight, reminding Maria of her one previous visit to these rooms. When the agent told her that the last tenant – an American art historian – had died the year before, Maria didn't say she had once met him in this place. Loose panes rattled as the agent opened the French doors to the terracotta terrace. Beside a speckled marble table, a shabby Cinzano parasol was folded down. The agent tried to raise it but the rusted hinges wouldn't yield. Maria's first meeting with the art historian was on this terrace. She'd seen a flyer for one of his lectures and wrote to him for advice on how to find an internship in America. They met on a spring day with some of the sharpness of winter still in the air. Jack Berman, a sturdy man in his mid-fifties, was wearing a blue blazer and a white cotton shirt.

'Don't call me Professor,' he told Maria. 'They all call me Professor – but there's no faculty here. It's a one-man show. I give lectures to pay the bills – every evening from now until fall.'

'It's beautiful here.'

'I got lucky – it's just right for these events. Did you study art history, Miss . . . ?'

'Manetti. Maria Manetti. Yes, I studied in Bologna.'

'And now, Miss Manetti, you want to see America.'

'My father says I should get some international experience. That I should work in a company for a while.'

'Good for him! Too many young people end up in museums. Nothing wrong with museums – but exposure to the business world is good when you're starting out.'

He took up the white envelope resting under an ashtray on the marble table.

'This letter is wonderful, but I didn't have time to read your résumé.'

He put on his black-rimmed glasses and read the first three paragraphs aloud.

'So many details for one so young!' he said, smiling. 'That's a good thing, by the way. I didn't have so many details when I was your age.'

'Maybe I should apply to an auction house?'

'They pay nothing. You'd just be answering the phone, moving things around – and smiling. They insist on that. I have a better plan.'

On the back of the envelope he wrote four lines that Maria would keep for the rest of her life.

Theodora Appel. Rare View. Alexandria. Virginia.

'It's a few miles from Washington. Theodora is an art dealer. She's a special friend. I'm over there in winter. Send her your résumé saying you've spoken to me.'

'Thank you,' said Maria, carefully folding the envelope.

'Theodora will like you – I can tell. She's always on the lookout for bright people. Rare View is her headquarters. And she has a gallery in New York. She has American interns your age – and an Italian restorer – one of the best in the business. He'll show you around – introduce you to some people.'

'Thank you very much.'

'It will be Theodora's decision. And if she takes you on, Ms Manetti, remember two things: never lie to her, and don't ask direct questions. She doesn't like direct questions. I found that out a long time ago. She'll teach you in her own way.'

'I had a professor like that in Bologna.'

'I should probably be more like that. But I'm not. That's why I like Theodora so much.'

He picked up a worn dossier with an embarrassed grin. 'I wonder if you could look at this? My residence permit ran out – and I need to send them an excuse. If you could check the Italian—'

'I'll do it now if you like.'

'There's no hurry – it's already overdue anyway. Do it on the train.'

'I'll post it to you tomorrow.'

'What part of Lombardy are you from?'

'Near Brescia.'

He stood up, his happy eyes purposeful.

'Come on – I want to show you something.'

She followed him through a broad salon with rows of wooden cinema seats, then along a passageway lined with books and records. He opened a door, gestured her inside and pointed upwards.

The estate agent threw open the shutters. Sparkling dust swirled in the brilliant winter light. Together they stared up at the frescoed map of Italy on the ceiling. The sea was aquamarine; mountains were shaded in earthen brown, plains in green. In the south-east, the oblique lines of an unfinished compass rose were outlined in faded sanguine beside an area of pure white where the fresco hadn't been completed or, perhaps, had fallen away over time. Was it this ceiling map that Theodora Appel wanted?

When Maria left the company, Appel asked her to periodically check the status of the apartment where she spent more than twenty summers. For Maria to report it for sale – to report the entire palazzo for sale – was to continue something from the past. This was the geography of the past. Maria resolved not to tell Appel. She wanted to protect her from further pain. In any case the four-storey building would be vastly expensive. But then the agent said something – almost to himself – as he gazed up at the magnificent painted ceiling.

'Strange you ask to see this.'

'Why?' asked Maria.

The cold urgency in her young voice made him sense some unknown but potentially valuable association.

'A man came here last week. This was the first room he asked to see.'

Appel had sent someone else. She already knew about the property. This was exactly in character. Every detail was checked and checked again. Maria's heart was pounding.

'He was a nice young man,' the agent continued, now scrutinising Maria's smooth face in a paternal way. 'An American.'

Maria ran her hand along the empty shelf in the passageway, then turned abruptly at the top of the stairway. But she didn't have to ask for a card. The agent held one out, the keys dangling from his fingers in the January light. She crossed the river at Santa Trinita shaking her head – almost saying something aloud. In the post office she stepped into one of the metallic phone booths and called Theodora Appel.

Maria glimpsed her breath in the freezing night air that surged into Rare View as she closed the door. It was dark, except for a halogen light over a panorama of Antwerp. The clock opposite read twenty past one. The hallway was the same as she remembered – formal yet homely. But it was the scent of Rare View that made her stop there in the hallway as her face slowly warmed. It was the scent of furniture polish and fresh flowers – and something else – some essence of the New World she could never place. She dropped the key into the deep pocket of her woollen coat, took off her shoes and walked through the darkened gallery. She could sleep on the sofa as she'd done many times after Appel's evenings with clients who were too important to come during the day. Then she heard a voice from the stairway.

'Maria! You're here!'

'Theodora!'

The two women embraced.

'Welcome back, Maria. I've missed you.'

'I've missed you too.'

Appel held Maria's hand. She had lost weight, and there were three silver strands in her auburn hair. If anything, she was more beautiful.

'I was so happy to hear from you, Maria. We've missed you. And thanks for the information – that reconnaissance you did for us.'

She opened the office door.

'You closed the partition,' said Maria.

'We'll open it again – now that you're back. I've got someone at your desk – but he's in the library most of the time.'

'I think I saw him outside.'

'He just came back from New York – the Winter Show.'

'The Winter Show! I always loved that one.'

'We'll do it together next year – you and I. Just like before.'

They sat down on the sofa.

'How are you, Theodora?'

'Things haven't been good. We lost a few people. We got sued. It's not the same – but I'm trying.'

'I'll help.'

'I know you will. We need to make some moves.'

Maria touched her wrist.

'You're wearing his watch.'

'It's too big,' said Appel.

'I love this room. Every detail is exactly as I remember. I learned everything in this room. Just like Jack said I would.'

'You knew plenty before he sent you over. Our Italian ambassador!'

'You put a new frame on the photograph of that fresco,' said Maria, getting up to look at it.

'How is the old place?' asked Appel, her throwaway tone not concealing a new and different note of tension, noticed by Maria.

'There's a lot of dust now. The plants are either dead or growing wild. The agent kept them a while, but he doesn't have the time. It's not the same—'

'I used to think Italy never changed,' said Appel with a thin smile.

'That place is not the same,' said Maria, her face now inches from the photograph of the ceiling map.

'You don't want me to buy it—'

'No, it's—'

'My dead lover's home.'

Appel's tone wasn't hard – just straight. It was the sort

of tone she used when narrowing a client's options – the moment a proposal turned into a negotiation. Although her assertion was sharp, Maria almost smiled with relief that this trait hadn't been dulled by her loss. The staff always said how good Maria was at handling – that's what they called it – Theodora Appel. She sat down again.

'It's a beautiful place. Of course it is. I just think—'

'You think it's not good for me.'

'The apartment is wonderful,' said Maria quietly. 'But since they're selling the whole palazzo – what would you do with it? And it is an enormous sum of money – even in America.'

'You're right, Maria. It's the past that costs us so much.'

VI

APPEL INTRODUCED THEM IN the library next morning. Maria wore jeans, a white linen shirt and a blue cardigan with pockets stretched deep. Kenji wore a two-piece charcoal suit and open white shirt.

'Kenji – this is Maria – from Italy.'

'I saw you last night,' said Maria. 'In the car.'

'I saw you too,' said Kenji. 'Pleased to meet you.'

'Did you like New York?'

'Yes, it is a great city.'

'Kenji had a terrific show,' said Appel. 'He has a way of finding things out. He joined us from Tokyo at the beginning of the year. He's translated our new catalogue – and we're already getting sales from Japan. We're thinking of opening a consignment office over there. Maybe a gallery.'

'Are you from Tokyo?' asked Maria.

'My city is called Mito. It is not far from Tokyo.'

'Mito?'

'Yes.'

'In Italian, *mito* means "myth".'

'You're going to learn a lot from Maria,' said Appel. 'She's an expert on all things European.'

'I have never been to Europe,' said Kenji.

'We'll all go together some day,' said Appel. 'Maria will be our guide.'

Kenji followed up on leads from the Winter Show, pursued contacts and transcribed Appel's dictaphone instructions from the booth at the Park Avenue Armory. The library resounded with her recorded voice, full of cool enthusiasm and clinical asides – a backstage commentary on the Winter Show. Kenji left blanks for the segments he couldn't understand. Maria periodically appeared in the arched entrance – sensing when he needed help transcribing Appel's words.

'Do you like her voice?'

'Yes, I do,' said Kenji.

'It's different . . .'

Maria stopped, realising he wouldn't understand. She meant different from before.

Maria also dealt with visitors when Appel was in New York. When a dealer insisted they photograph maps he wanted to sell, Maria obliged. But when the man left, she flicked open the empty case. 'There's no film,' she said. 'We don't buy from people like that.'

'Maria saved the company,' said Klara. She was smoking

with Kenji on the back porch at Rare View – a ritual she established after the Winter Antiques Show. Appel stopped smoking years before. 'Thea spent three months in Florence after Jack Berman died. Everything was done by phone through Maria and me. Not even the New York director had the number. Maria finally got Thea to come back by returning to Italy herself. She flew over there and said she needed time with her family. That brought Thea to her senses.'

Colleagues didn't ask Maria why she left or why she returned. They presumed it was arranged between herself and Appel. And when she moved back to her old apartment building in Georgetown, they spoke of her time away as a sabbatical. Although Kenji couldn't predict the impact of Maria's return on his role in the company, he presumed that Appel would now accelerate her plans for Tokyo. It would be pointless to ask her for a visa if she intended to send him back to Japan. In a letter to his parents he even wrote that he might be back for cherry blossom.

Klara told the Rare View staff it was Kenji who persuaded Maria to come back to the company. When two of the salesmen met him the day after Maria came back, they grinned quizzically as though meeting him for the first time. They were glad he was there, but he didn't know why. Kenji tried to imagine the first words between the two women after Maria walked carefully across the carpet of snow and opened the Rare View door with a key of her own.

On the Saturday after their first meeting Maria arrived at the guest house wearing a white scarf over the lower half of her face.

'I'm going to the workshop in Washington – we do all the restoration and framing there. Want to come?'

'I'd like that. I'll get my coat.'

'This place is so empty,' said Maria, stepping inside. 'They should get more furniture. And something for the walls.'

'I like it.'

'The atrium makes it so cold.'

'I spend most of the time at Rare View. It's warm there. So I don't mind.'

They got into the Transit and Maria started the engine.

'What kind of visa do you have?'

'A tourist visa,' said Kenji. 'For ninety days.'

'I used to have one of those. Do you have a driving licence?'

'I have an international one,' he said.

'How long is left?'

'About six weeks.'

'Be careful. And if you're stopped, don't say you work for Theodora. Think of something else.'

They parked in an icy concrete yard. Kenji followed her up a metal stairway and into the fluorescent-lighted workshop. Frame samples of maple, walnut, cedar and teak hung in the phosphorescent space.

'Theodora calls this the "backstage". She tells us to bring clients here to select frames,' said Maria. 'We have hundreds of mouldings – and we can copy any museum frame they want. Then we show them the mat designs that cover the edge of the map. Every border is painted by hand. Some clients want the full sheet displayed – with no margin covered by the mat. We call this floating.'

They passed a workbench where a woman sprayed liquid chalk onto a wooden frame.

'Gesso,' said Maria. 'It's the base for gold leaf. And over here is the acrylic glass – for ultraviolet light protection. The colour will fade under ordinary glass.'

'Is it always open on Saturdays?' asked Kenji.

'There are no fixed hours. Some prefer to work at night – especially after the Winter Show. Theodora doesn't care, as long as the orders get done. And workshop staff are on commission – we're the only gallery that does that.'

The six sheets of the great de'Barbari view of Venice lay on an adjacent table.

'I saw it in New York—'

'Yes,' said Maria. 'Lewis Peters bought it – but he didn't like the frame.'

'Venice must be beautiful,' said Kenji. 'I would—'

'Did you like Mr Peters?'

'I spoke to him for a few minutes—'

'Did you like him?'

'I'm not sure.'

'I don't like him,' said Maria.

'Why?'

'He tried something – with me.' She lingered on the map for a moment. 'Theodora once told me she'd never do business with him again. But she's changed her mind.'

'Why did she change her mind?'

'I don't know. Come on – the restoration lab is over here.'

Kenji followed her through the beige swing doors, instantly recognising the light scent of acetone. The restored gores of a globe were drying on a fine nylon line. A restorer was manipulating a submerged map in a shallow tray.

'*Ciao*, Palmiro – this is Kenji.'

'Oh, hello!' said the man, with a friendly emphasis that indicated he'd already heard about Kenji. Palmiro was a thin man of about fifty, wearing a white laboratory coat and a faded tweed cap. They switched to Italian. Kenji gazed down at the Hondius map of America submerged in the shallow liquid. Boats and sea creatures shimmered in the Pacific under the glow of a single yellow bulb. There were foxing spores at the top of the sheet and brown lines left by the margins of an old frame. Palmiro turned it over. Kenji had seen this procedure many times in the laboratory at Waseda University. He enjoyed the musical murmur of the words he couldn't understand.

'How is it over there?' asked Palmiro.

'It was strange at first,' said Maria. 'It's better now.'

'How does she seem? To you, I mean?'

'The same – and not the same. It's understandable.'

'People keep their distance,' he said. 'From grief.'

'I noticed – except for Klara.'

'Why did you come back?'

Maria hesitated.

'It was the tone of her voice – when I called from Italy about that property. She sounded – I don't know – vulnerable. I never heard that before.'

'The palazzo with the fresco?'

'Theodora's obsessed with that place. I'd like you to see it one day – get your opinion.'

'I'll try to visit next time I'm in Italy.'

He looked up at her face.

'You're pale.'

'I'm always pale,' she said quickly.

'Angels are always pale. You're her angel.'

'I have a job that I like.'

'You have a mission.'

'She needs me.'

Maria turned to Kenji and spoke in English.

'The rice tape we use is from Japan.'

His gaze was still fixed, trance-like, on the shallow sea.

'He's concentrating,' said Palmiro in Italian.

'He's somewhere else,' said Maria with a smile.

'You like him. He's your new challenge.'

Maria touched Kenji's arm.

'The rice tape we use is from Japan.'

'It's acid-free,' said Kenji.

'We'll make it look like it was,' said Maria.

'Not too new,' said Palmiro.

'Sometime between then and now,' she said, pushing on the laboratory door.

'*Ciao*, Palmiro. *Grazie*.'

'Maria—'

'Yes – I forgot,' she said, taking a manila envelope from her satchel. She tipped two parts of a torn black-and-white photograph onto the smooth workbench. In the first fragment a man stood beside a large brass telescope. The second was an urban panorama of belfries and terracotta roofs. Maria gently put them together.

'Theodora took this at La Specola in Florence. It's the observatory – the best view in the city.'

Kenji leaned over.

'Her professor.'

In early March scattered snowdrops began to bloom outside the library window. Appel declared the Winter Show a great success and instructed the interns to increase the price of the rarest maps by ten per cent. 'It's called the price discovery mechanism,' she told Kenji, 'and New York pointed us up. We have two options: to hold or to increase. We never lower the price of these maps. We can offer some clients ten per cent – but this is already priced in.'

At Rare View Maria quietly resumed her role as Appel's go-between. She answered complex questions and gave the salesmen anecdotes and short narratives to help them sell maps: 'Most of our maps were once owned by aristocrats, prelates and scholarly bibliophiles – clients love to hear that. Blaeu's wall maps are rare because so many were damaged hanging from wooden rods. There are less than a thousand maps in the world from before the fourteenth century.' Maria understood cartography in historical context, while Appel needed to understand the technical and graphical details of every map. From these elements she built a story. Maria already had stories. Appel's business manoeuvres were skilful but complex, and it was one of Maria's tasks to patiently explain to salesmen why delayed payments reduced commissions, why stock needed to be repriced and at what point Appel should be involved in negotiations with clients. Some of the salesmen even called her Appel's translator. The partition between Appel's office and the antechamber was thrown open again. Maria had no sales targets and no job title. She worked to her own schedule and assisted with the company's most important clients: a billionaire near Charlottesville, a curator at Colonial Williamsburg and the president of a media company in Manhattan.

Maria was assuming more responsibility – and was

behind the dismissal of one of the salesmen. At first Kenji didn't realise what was happening. The man was selecting maps for the Pittsburgh Antiques Show when Appel called him to the office. Klara, Kenji and an intern were working on the client list.

'You're taking a lot to Pittsburgh, Joe,' Appel said in a tone so calm it sounded like a compliment.

'Yes, well, there's a lot of old money—'

'You still have a chart over there from last year – don't you?'

'No. There's nothing I recall—'

'With a client.'

'No. We brought—'

'You're fired, Joe.'

The man laughed, expecting Appel to say something else. But she was silent. He stepped towards the desk.

'There's nothing I know about – and even if—'

'Nothing you know about?' Appel repeated. 'We've just called them – it's been on consignment for a year.'

'You know how many—'

'No consignments of more than thirty days without my signature. You know the rules. We don't like things going missing.'

Kenji scrutinised the man's incredulous expression.

'It's over, Joe. Get out.'

That evening Maria came to the library, car keys tinkling in the deep pocket of her woollen coat. Unlike Appel's visits, during which she moved constantly, Maria sat down on the ornate chair beside Kenji's desk.

'The stock tracking has broken down.'

'But you're doing it now so—'

'Things have changed. A lot of things. Maps have been moved from client to client. The salesmen here call it "fishing". That chart was not in the ledger. It's $150,000 – now worth ten per cent more. I told Thea I wasn't sure if it was a mistake. She told me he'd been caught. She was careful not to accuse him – you saw that.'

'Did you know him well?'

'Not very well. This wouldn't have happened if the system still worked. That's why she asked me to check everything. I found there had been a lot of discounting. Discounts mean higher turnover – and higher commissions. Everyone was doing it – so I just told Thea in a general kind of way. But the missing map—'

'It will get better now,' said Kenji. 'Because you're here.'

'Thea is distracted. I understand that. She hasn't been paying attention. And now she's working on some big deal.'

'Is it from the Winter Show?'

'It's Mr Peters. He's coming down here in a few days.'

Appel came to the library the following morning.

'You're going to Pittsburgh,' she told Kenji. 'I need Maria here – the others have appointments. Don't worry – call in if you need help. Tell them stories about Rare View. This business is about stories. Just make it up – that's what Maria does. Use me. That's what I'm here for. Make them feel like insiders.'

Kenji loaded the Transit with print racks, booth lamps, catalogues, certificates of authenticity, headed stationery, a dictaphone, extension cords and a wooden map chest. The opening night of the Pittsburgh Antiques Show, held at the Allegheny Country Club, turned out to be more formal than the opening night of the New York Winter Antiques Show. Most of the men wore tuxedos – Kenji wore a business suit and tie. He phoned the client who had the map on consignment. Within an hour a woman of about forty arrived at the booth.

'Thank you for your patience. It's a beautiful piece. But my husband and I have decided not to buy it.'

Kenji rested the framed Mediterranean chart on the wooden chest in the centre of the booth.

'Thank you. I will tell Miss Appel.'

The woman looked around the booth as though about to ask about something – or somebody – else.

'Is that all?' she asked nervously.

'Pardon me?'

'Is there something I need to sign or—'

'No, madam,' said Kenji, still examining the chart. 'That is all. Thank you.'

It was after nine when Kenji returned to the hotel and sat

at the bar. Since his arrival in America he'd been drinking less – not because of any change in his desire for alcohol, but because there were fewer opportunities to socialise in the suburban environs of Alexandria. Two dealers from the New York show recognised him and insisted on buying dinner. It was only when he woke the next morning that Kenji remembered the accent he struggled to understand. 'And what's going on with 57th Street?' the other asked. 'I heard the gallery might be for sale. Is she short of cash?' Kenji recalled something Klara told him. 'Everyone knows something about Theodora Appel.' He would hear many stories from dealers jealous of her success. They said she had no friends in the trade. She was selling stock before she bought it. She married an American fugitive in Italy.

Kenji sold nothing in Pittsburgh. But when he phoned Rare View, Appel made a point of congratulating him on retrieving the map. 'That could have gone wrong, you know – sometimes it's the bad people who call the police.' She said he could build on the contacts he'd made. Her unexpected loyalty – or pity for his failure to sell anything – filled him with contempt for the dealers he had met.

'And I think we may have a client for the map you recovered. He's in Virginia. You can drop it off on the way back.'

Kenji was content to be given this task. He understood that the stock, clients and staff were being directed according to a logic understood only by Appel and, perhaps, Maria. Important decisions were taken off-stage. He sensed he was valued by the woman he couldn't yet understand. He remembered what Curtis Hahn told him in New York: 'We're relieved she's found someone like you.'

Dandelions grew in the fields beside the driveway to a colonial mansion near Orange, Virginia. Kenji followed the client into the spacious living room and fitted a picture light. The bulb cast a soft glow on the smooth vellum. Appel had persuaded the client to take the Mediterranean chart on loan while coming to a decision. Maria explained her method. 'She doesn't want to see clients until they decide. It's our job to keep in touch while they're making up their minds.'

When he returned to Washington, Kenji was stunned by the explosion of cherry blossoms. He'd seen pictures of the lantern-lighting ceremony in a guidebook Klara gave him on his first day at work. But he never imagined the impact of his country's blossoms on the monumental core of the city. At the Jefferson Memorial and around the Tidal Basin, white Yoshino swayed in the breeze. Along the great boulevards the ranked trees reminded him of the cherry viewings in Ueno Park. Every year the gallery staff assembled there for evening picnics. As a junior in the art department he'd been sent out during the short season of blossoms to mark the geography of friendship with canvas and rugs. Kenji glanced at his watch as it turned dark. He stopped abruptly when he saw the date. His American visa had expired. He'd been too busy to think about this inevitable deadline. It had come and gone. Yet he was strangely relieved by this expiry. The time beyond – whatever it might bring – would be his own. When he arrived at Rare View he poured a glass of whisky in the kitchen and went barefoot to the library. He flicked through a new five-volume edition of the *Portugaliae Monumenta Cartographica*, left on a map chest for him to classify. On a double-column page he read the translation of a 1526 letter by Charles V exhorting his cosmographers to 'make a nautical chart and world map or round sphere on which are located all the islands and continents discovered up to now and that will be discovered from now on'.

VII

K ENJI WAS WOKEN BY a helicopter landing on the Rare View lawn. He gazed up from the library carpet where he'd slept. The morning light threw shadow blades onto the ceiling and, for an instant, he saw his father's face through a spoked wheel in the bicycle shop. He wanted to light a cigarette and watch the smoke drift up to the spinning blades. There were businesslike footsteps on the bare boards of the hallway outside, but he was sure they wouldn't come into the library. He got up and went to the window. A pilot stood beside the helicopter. The man they were waiting for had arrived.

'We've been calling the guest house,' Klara said sharply when Kenji went to the antechamber. 'Where's that inventory you've been working on?'

'It's here,' said Kenji, taking it from a high shelf. 'I was sorting the books that arrived while I was in Pittsburgh.'

'Thea's with Mr Peters – you'll be joining them later.'

Kenji looked at the slow-turning blades outside the

window. He tried to imagine their approach from Washington – a short flight south over the Potomac and the old town. They would have searched for Rare View at the end of the driveway, surrounded by a manicured lawn extending to the thick shrubs and the treeline. The most visible feature would have been the red Momiji tree – standing like a target outside Appel's window. Just after noon, while Kenji was smoking on the back porch, Klara told him to join the meeting. Appel was speaking as he entered the main gallery.

'. . . and art outperformed the stock market by seven per cent last year. We're right in the middle of this – and we've got the best stock in America. The client list alone is worth a fortune. Twenty-five years of the best contacts in the business.'

The circular table was covered with the rarest portolan navigation charts and printed maps. There were three atlases – among them the Ortelius *Theatre of the World*, propped open at the map of Iceland. Two large globes stood either side of the fireplace which – for the first time since Kenji arrived – was lit with aromatic wood. Everyone was standing. Peters moved slowly around the table, occasionally looking directly at Appel with the intimidating intensity of a man who was used to being in control. Kenji stood near the door. Among those who buy, he once heard Appel say, there was great competition to invest well. The acquisition of sub-standard or overpriced material was a sign of poor connoisseurship.

'We're also putting together a major exhibition for New York,' Appel continued, suddenly motioning towards Kenji. 'It's his idea.'

A leaf of the atlas slipped gently from Peters's fingers as he looked at Kenji.

'I believe you met at the Winter Show,' said Appel.

'Yes, I remember.'

'Kenji will be running our new office in Tokyo.'

'Congratulations,' said Peters.

'It's a pleasure to meet you again,' said Kenji.

'The exhibition won't be at the New York gallery,' Appel continued. 'We're going for something bigger. We'll show our best items – and a selection of maps we've placed with museums and libraries.'

'Where do you have in mind?' Peters asked Appel, still looking at Kenji's expressionless face.

'We're hoping for the AT&T Tower on Madison Avenue – in September. We're taking the whole lot to Japan after that. Kenji has incredible contacts – and he organised a landmark exhibition there last year. It was all over the Tokyo papers. No western map gallery is even close. Japan will generate very substantial returns.'

They crossed the hallway to Appel's office. A caterer in a white jacket stood beside a circular table set for three. The partition was closed and Appel's office looked strangely small – even though this was how Kenji had seen it on the day of his interview. He made to leave, thinking they would be dining with someone more important – maybe the sales director. But Appel gripped Kenji's elbow and guided him to the table. The third seat was for him. Then he noticed the two inventory dossiers in the centre of the table. He had worked on these with Maria. As the waiter served, Appel and Peters talked about the market and people Kenji had never met. He listened attentively, gradually under-standing that after Peters bought the de'Barbari view of Venice, Appel proposed an investment partnership. Peters would finance the acquisition of new stock and receive a generous return as maps were sold. Kenji wondered if this new money would be used to finance the company's office in Tokyo. That might explain his presence at the lunch. He thought back to the booth in New York and how uncom-promising Appel had been with the decorator. This must have been to impress Peters, just as her performance earlier had been. Peters was now more of a partner than a client. She called him 'our associate'. The visit to Rare View was Appel's opportunity to show him how his investment was being used.

Appel picked up the Rare View inventory and asked Kenji to tell them about it. He explained the cost and average margin for different categories of stock. He listed the main differences between Rare View and New York and compared turnover times between the two locations. For Peters, maps were just another business – but he was gradually learning about cartographic history. He told them of a recent trip to London where he visited the map room at the Foreign Office. He'd also seen the great 1541 Mercator globe at the Greenwich maritime museum. As Appel shared her memories of London she occasionally glanced at Kenji, who sensed she was glad he was there. As a young dealer Appel had spent hours working out the classification system of the library at the Royal Geographical Society – arranged by donor rather than as a single collection. She told them about an all-day meeting with London print dealers shortly after she launched her own business.

'I remember we haggled the whole day. Afterwards they took me to a bar – a pub – called the Pillars of Hercules. Although I wasn't a heavy drinker, I matched them round for round. I regretted it afterwards. I had a nasty fall in the lane beside Christina Foyle's bookstore.'

By casually presenting such episodes Appel drew clients into her confidence. But to Kenji these stories seemed concocted. Her murmured reflections while stooped over maps seemed more authentic and sincere. Appel told Peters about other collections he might like to visit. She smiled towards Kenji as she described Samuel Pepys's copy of the *Atlas Japannensis* at Cambridge, the leather panoramas at the Topkapi and the globes at the Jagiellonian University in Krakow. 'Maria came on that trip – she knows so much about cartography – it's amazing.'

There was a small pause at the mention of this name – as

though Appel had said too much, or forgotten some point of etiquette.

'Have you heard from her?' asked Peters hesitantly.

'She's back working for us!'

Kenji noticed a flicker of incomprehension on Peters's face. Maria had been assigned to him when he first became a client. Although he was now dealing directly with the owner of the company, he seemed to take Maria's absence as a slight.

'She's in New York today,' said Appel. 'We're going to Florence in June because there's a big map exhibition at the Medici Library. We want to see how it's presented. It'll help us prepare for our September exhibition in New York.' Then she changed the subject. 'What are they saying in London about the Hereford map offer?'

Kenji read about this in the *Map Collector*. The thirteenth-century Hereford map – a large illuminated manuscript – had been consigned to auction to help finance the restoration of the cathedral where it was housed. But it was withdrawn when more than 10,000 petitioners objected to the sale. The map's future was now uncertain. A company called Mappa Mundi was offering 7,450 shares at £1,000 each. The plan was to save the map from auction. Peters had a copy of the prospectus.

'It will fail,' he said tersely. 'Shareholders won't actually get anything – except a useless share certificate and a facsimile. But the idea of a syndication is not bad. You could split one of those atlases, for example – then at least everyone would get something.'

Kenji was still shocked by this suggestion as he watched them walk across the lawn. He peered at the Momiji tree, relieved that it was unscathed by the draught of the helicopter blades. The caterers cleared the table in Appel's office and Kenji reopened the partition. He sat at his desk in the library, feeling light-headed from the rich western food and wine. For a moment he thought he might faint, as he did once during a baseball game at school in Mito. He walked through the silent house, then returned to the main gallery where the maps and atlases from the presentation were abandoned on the table. He wrote down the prices of the items Peters had seen. The total was just over seven million dollars. He now realised that Appel was pretending the great atlas and the other items were new acquisitions. To Kenji they now assumed a strange status – a phantom collection within the company stock. As the helicopter rose over Rare View he wondered what Appel had done – or what she intended to do – with her associate's money.

It was dusk when Kenji parked the car outside the guest house. There was a light in the hallway. Sometimes salesmen from New York arrived unannounced. But when he opened the door, Maria was sitting on the sofa.

'I hope I didn't startle you,' she said.

'I thought you were in New York today.'

'No, I stayed here – in case Thea needed details.' Kenji noticed a thick dossier on the sofa beside her. 'She called a couple of times for prices. She told me you were a great help – with the inventory.'

'Most of it was your work. I don't know why—'

'I couldn't face that man.'

Kenji thought for a moment.

'Does she need his money for Tokyo?'

Maria stood up and walked towards the atrium. 'I don't know. I don't know what's going on.'

'Would you like something?'

'Thank you. I've already eaten – that's why I stayed late.' She took her coat from the rack.

'If you have a moment, Maria – I'd like to ask you something.'

'Yes?'

'It's about my visa,' he said in a quiet, confessional tone. 'It expired last week.'

'I wouldn't worry about it,' she said with a light, tired voice. 'We can organise a trip – something for a renewal. Thea has been talking about visiting Italy.'

'Should I speak to her?'

'No. I'll see what I can do. And if there's any trouble,

we need to say it's my fault. Some administrative mistake. You understand?'

'Yes, I understand.'

She walked towards the door, and then turned.

'You left very early this morning.'

'Pardon me?'

'I got here just before seven – but the car was gone.'

'I slept in the library at Rare View. I was tired.'

'Oh, I see,' she said with a small laugh. 'I thought you had a girlfriend already! Good night, Kenji. And don't worry about the visa.'

VIII

THE ASSEMBLY – AN annual meeting of company staff – was held the day after Lewis Peters's visit to Rare View. The proximity of these events created a sense of change that was heightened when, late in the afternoon, Appel announced that the New York gallery would be relocating from 57th Street to 76th Street. The stunned staff listened in silence. Then the New York salesmen began to question the move; there would be fewer walk-in sales, thousands of clients would have to be notified, office space would be reduced. Appel responded with arguments that Kenji often heard her use on the phone: 'This is a niche business. The client list has too much dead wood. We're art dealers – not retailers. We don't need a big window on the street.' Kenji noticed how the men from New York – there were no women – seemed sceptical of her in a way Kenji hadn't noticed at the rarefied Winter Antiques Show. They all spoke, except for Curtis Hahn. Appel was being challenged. But she was calm, insisting the New York gallery should become more like Rare View. 'But we don't have a fireplace!' someone joked. Nobody laughed.

In mid-April, Appel sent Kenji and the Rare View driver to New York. They were needed to help with the new gallery. Kenji was unsure why he'd been sent, and wondered about Appel's motives for moving the gallery uptown. They picked up an intern at the 57th Street gallery and drove to the new location off Madison Avenue. An architect sitting at a desk in the middle of the empty space told them the internal walls could be knocked through to increase natural light. This was one of Appel's priorities – to better show the original colouring of her maps. Although Kenji noticed how his two colleagues deferred to him, he joined in the manual labour to help Appel's demanding schedule. They breached the dividing walls with sledgehammers and loaded the van with bricks and broken sheetrock. After a slow drive through Queens they arrived at a dump in Long Island City and paid to unload the rubble themselves.

At night Kenji slept in the empty space on cushions from a discarded sofa. The architect told him he could use the showers in a gymnasium on First Avenue by entering through the reception-area toilets. He assured Kenji no one would check for membership – he designed the place himself. Beside his makeshift accommodation Kenji placed an alarm clock and a telephone with an extension cord running the length of the empty space. A soft lamp at the back of the building shone through the bare windows. When he lay down it reminded him of his room in Mito.

The demolition work and trips to Long Island continued for another week. One of the final tasks was the removal of the old spotlight fittings. While the intern was prising one loose, a section of plaster burst from the ceiling, hitting him on the forehead. As they drove to the hospital on 68th Street, Kenji held a roll of paper towel to stem the bleeding. A doctor stitched the wound and told the intern not to work for a week. Kenji and the driver returned to the new gallery – the tradesmen were due the following day. Their final task was to widen the doorway in the only remaining partition. They used the Rare View chainsaw from the van. Kenji held back the exposed wires as the driver slowly cut into the sheetrock. Dust and masonry scattered across the floor. They took turns on the ladder, lifting the heavy saw to cut the upper sections of the partition. Kenji was working towards the ceiling, his head beside a temporary construction lamp, when they arrived. Appel and Maria looked up at the two bare-chested men. In the deafening noise Kenji didn't turn. The last slab of sheetrock smashed to the floor and the piercing chainsaw cut short. The sudden silence was filled with the pleasant scent of petrol.

'Have you been to the Frick Collection?' Appel asked.

Kenji stared down from the ladder with blank surprise. He didn't answer.

'The Morgan Library?'

His hoarse words came louder than intended.

'No, we've had a lot—'

'Why not?' she asked. 'What have you been doing?'

Kenji wondered why the two women had come so late. Perhaps they'd been to dinner with a client or to an evening auction.

'How are you going to organise an exhibition if you don't go to any?'

'I did not have time,' Kenji replied.

'We got the AT&T on Madison. Wrapped it up today.'

'It's a beautiful space,' said Maria.

'What will it be anyway?' Appel asked. 'We're going to need a theme for the exhibition.'

Kenji was unprepared.

'Progress in cartography,' he said.

'The progress you see is not what they saw,' said Appel, admiring the smooth edge they'd cut in the sheetrock.

'We should show how maps get better,' said Kenji.

'Is accuracy a kind of progress? Is that your idea?'

'Cartography is a progression,' he said defiantly. He wished he'd spoken like this to the director in Tokyo. His theme could still redeem what happened. Appel paced towards the back of the gallery. She turned back when she saw his bedding on the floor.

'Don't you understand – those maps capture time,' she

said. 'They are maps of then, when maps had a cosmos, unlike now.'

Kenji was silent. The driver put on his jacket as though leaving an argument in someone else's family. When he opened the door the naked construction bulbs swung in the cold draught. Kenji's disoriented shadow lurched around the walls of the empty space. When he glanced at her, Maria closed her woollen coat. Kenji tried to concentrate. He was light-headed from the din of the chainsaw against the partition and his mouth was dry from the dust and fumes. Why were they challenging his deeply held conviction? They were probing – testing the viability of his idea with synchronised arguments. Maybe they had something to drink on Madison Avenue.

'Cartography is a science,' said Kenji, putting on a leather jacket. 'Mapmakers wanted to be right.'

'Maps show the richness of their time,' said Appel. 'The exhibition should illuminate their world.'

'But they were wrong,' said Kenji. 'California was not an island.'

'Those cartographers were concerned with more than geographical realism,' said Maria. 'They set down their beliefs, their fears, their dreams.'

'Each map is a timestamp,' said Appel. 'And I almost forgot; that film producer bought two maps – a hundred thousand. Four thousand of that is yours. He liked California as an island.'

Her tone made it seem like a game. Was she teasing, or mocking him?

'The imaginary islands of Lake Superior. The City of Crystal in New England.'

At Rare View she spoke like this when she was tired.

'Remember the old cartographer's rule? Distance, direction, shape. When making a map – one of those is always lost.'

Appel opened the door and turned back.

'Go to some of the big collections. We've sold them lots of beautiful things. You'll get ideas for the exhibition. Maria – you did a tour like that a few years ago – what did you call it?'

'Survey Americana.'

'That's it!' said Appel. 'This will be your Survey Americana, Kenji. And don't leave New York without seeing the Medici portrait at the Frick Collection – it's by an artist called Pontormo. It's been on loan there for decades. I found out tonight it's going to be auctioned off.'

Kenji stood alone in the empty gallery. He'd stumbled into some grotesque version of his original idea. What would he do with the maps he'd carefully set aside for the exhibition? And the multiple editions of the *American Coast Pilot* – slim handbooks in red bindings giving distances between harbours along the Atlantic? Each volume carried an invitation for navigators to contribute improvements for future editions. Kenji intended to show these as he'd shown the three Nagakubo maps in Tokyo – each one a testament to progress. Now, with his world view abruptly contradicted, he no longer knew where to begin. The bulbs hung still. In the white dust there were footprints to the door. The perspiration on his chest had mixed with gypsum dust and dried like liquid chalk. He would go to the gymnasium on First Avenue – maybe he'd get a beer – but first he needed to rest.

The tapping was soft but insistent. He dismissed it without opening his eyes and drifted again. Then it came back. He woke with a jolt, frightened. Someone knew he was there. The bedding couldn't be seen from the street. He had read about moments like this in the Japanese newspapers. Breathless accounts of how life could end at an American doorstep. He stood up and zipped the leather jacket to his chin. The tapping of a key, or a coin, started again. He peered around the partition, his hand on the smooth edge of the sheetrock. She looked the same as the first moment he'd seen her – the beams of passing cars on her pale face. He opened the door.

'I'm sorry about all that talk,' said Maria. 'Thea is not herself these days.'

'Where is she?'

'At the hotel – she's tired.'

'I'm going to First Avenue,' said Kenji, locking the door. 'I'll walk you over.'

'Where were you – before coming here?'

'We had dinner with one of the AT&T executives. Thea wanted to explain the exhibition idea.'

'Did you know she was going to sell the gallery on 57th Street?'

'She told me the night before.'

'Why is she doing that?'

'I don't know. The new gallery will be smaller than 57th Street.'

'She's raising money.'

'Yes – but I don't think it's for Tokyo.'

At the Frick Collection Kenji sat beside the fountain in the inner cloister, thinking about the arguments at the empty gallery. Appel had elevated his exhibition idea, but she'd taken away his leitmotif of progress. It never occurred to him that here – in the New World – anyone could possibly question this theme. At first he had been embarrassed by Maria's late-night return to the gallery. But her reassurance was soft and for the first time he wondered if she had another motive. He studied Vermeer's *Officer and a Laughing Girl* with its faithfully painted Blaeu wall map in the background. He found the 'Halberdier' portrait that Appel so admired. The young Florentine, identified as a Medici duke, stood before a strange nocturnal fortification holding a halberd pike – his gaze not precisely focused nor his appearance impressed. Then he heard those words again.

'It's quite magnificent.'

'I've always loved this place,' said a second man. 'When I came with my father, the staff used to give us coffee and soda – it was like a private mansion.'

'You lived around here?' asked Peters.

'Two blocks over. Park Avenue.'

'A classy neighbourhood.'

Kenji froze in front of the Halberdier, staring at the youthful, unflinching face. He should have turned to signal his presence – to avoid the impression that he was listening to their conversation. But it was too late. He would do what he had done in Mito and Tokyo – stand trance-like until nobody noticed him anymore.

'So you'll think about it,' said Peters.

'We'll consider it. Very seriously.'

'And the board?'

'Not my decision,' the man said quickly. 'There's a lot of politics.'

'I understand,' said Peters.

'I'm not saying they'll say no. It's just that they're careful about—'

'There's nothing wrong with my money.'

'Of course not, Lewis. But you know what they're like around here. It's more about—'

'Breeding – reputation.'

'I didn't say that.'

'I know, Marcus. But it's what they think.'

'I'll see what I can do, Lewis.'

'Thank you. I appreciate your support.'

From his pocket Kenji took out the only piece of paper he had – a worn floorplan of Appel's new gallery. He began to transcribe the text beside the painting of the Halberdier.

'You must have quite a collection by now.'

'Not bad,' said Peters. 'But since the divorce – I'm missing one piece.'

They laughed coarsely.

'You're a handsome guy, Lewis! You'll have no problem.'

Kenji tried to imagine them at the far side of the gallery behind him. Peters would be fashionably dressed, his hair with the sheen of a squash player after a hard game. The other man would be shorter and older. Maybe holding a pair of suede gloves. Unlike Peters, he would avoid eye contact.

'Collecting is like the hunt,' said Peters as they exited within feet of Kenji's left shoulder.

They laughed again.

'I must tell you who I met in London.'

For a moment, Kenji thought to follow them. But he remained still, staring at the picture, his heart pounding.

On the train to Connecticut Kenji wondered if he should ask to see the Vinland map. He was still undecided as he marvelled at the six-storey book tower in the Beinecke Library at Yale. The Vinland map was discovered by a

New Haven book dealer in 1957. The parchment was said to date from around 1440. When Yale University Press published a book about the map – on the eve of Columbus Day 1965 – the biggest cartographical controversy of the twentieth century began. 'In fact,' Appel told Kenji before he left on his Survey Americana, 'the controversy began before publication – they didn't release review copies of that book.' On the map, a place called 'Vinilanda Insula' was shown west of Greenland. If it were genuine, the map would be the earliest known representation of the land that became America. In the library at Rare View Kenji had seen a facsimile – also published by Yale – with the original receipt for fifteen dollars. And on the day of his interview he'd seen the clipping from the *Washington Post*: 'America of Vikings Shown on Pre-Columbian Map'.

The Vinland map was donated to Yale by Paul Mellon, who bought it from the New Haven book dealer. Its provenance was shrouded in secrecy, and experts immediately disagreed about its authenticity. At a Washington conference in 1966 a participant suggested that the dealer – who refused to give details of the map's history – write down everything he knew about its previous ownership. Such testimony would only be read after his death. With each passing moment of Kenji's privileged access to the Yale collections, he felt more anxious about asking to see the controversial map. He was almost relieved when the librarian asked about Appel's new catalogue. She had called ahead about this. Perhaps there were some items the university would consider for purchase. Although Kenji knew he was a pawn in Appel's strategy, he also felt she was proud of him – as though he too were an acquisition that clients should see. He didn't ask to see the Vinland map.

Kenji's Survey Americana continued at the John Carter Brown Library in Providence. Appel gave him the catalogue of the bicentennial exhibition organised there – *The Italians and the Creation of America*. All the exhibits were from the library's own collections and she had marked the maps he should see. At the University of Southern Maine he exchanged a copy of his Tokyo exhibition booklet for a catalogue of an exhibition about Norumbega – a mythical land shiftingly represented on maps of the American north-east. When he returned to Grand Central Terminal after his ten-day Survey Americana, Kenji gazed up at the ceiling of the concourse coated in seven decades of grime. He struggled to see the painted constellations he read about in his guidebook, but as the minutes passed he was sure he could see them, or imagine how they once had been.

The Appel Galleries – the official name of the company – was stencilled in gold leaf on the window of the property Kenji had last seen as an empty shell. He opened the door, deactivated the alarm and stepped into the flickering light. There was a note from Appel on the reception desk; he should get in touch with the logistics manager at the AT&T building. There would be no inaugural reception at the new gallery – she didn't want to diminish the impact of his exhibition. This expectation made Kenji anxious. He walked through the new gallery with its compact spaces and alcoves for the map chests, racks and desks. Then he reactivated the alarm, closed the door and gazed back into the new space, slowly realising what was missing: the embracing Venetian chandelier from the old gallery on 57th Street.

In the following days Kenji updated the inventory and checked the location of maps under consideration in clients' homes and offices. This exercise provided an opportunity to make selections for his exhibition. He spent an afternoon trying to find the American Geographical Society, intending to investigate the stained-glass maps he read about at Rare View. He wanted to borrow the Tiffany era copy of Waldseemüller's world map of 1507 – the first to use the word 'America' – so he could mount it in a light box at his exhibition. It would be a perfect introduction to rare maps. But when he arrived at 156th Street, the building had been converted into a college. He showed the caretaker a photograph in the booklet, but the man told him he was in the wrong place, there were no stained-glass maps in the building. The Society had relocated ten years previously – Kenji should enquire at the new location on Wall Street. But his search was interrupted when he met Maria at the gallery. First she told him about her afternoon with a client called 'the Captain'. Then she told him how Appel's plans had changed.

Five framed charts were propped against the wall of the spacious Fifth Avenue living room when Maria arrived. Captain Bonne, a retired naval officer, was one of Appel's first clients. Maria usually hung maps on her own – sometimes with an interior decorator – but seldom with a client. As she prepared to measure the wall, the Captain said the surface had been glazed by an artist from Miami. She doubted it would be possible to place each of ten nails accurately first time. She usually hammered a second if the first were wrong. But the Captain was confident.

'Leave ten inches between the bottom of the frame and the top of the sofa,' he said. 'Measure three down from the top and allow for the swing.'

The Captain took a cigar stub from his desk. He was the same height as Maria, with the sinuous physique of a distance runner. He sharpened a pencil with a fruit knife and leaned in to mark the wall. Maria hammered the nails. The first chart hung straight. They moved to the second and marked the points. 'Nail it,' he said, lighting the cigar. He calculated the position of the centre map. Again the points were precise. She eagerly followed his method – for the first time believing the others could be exact.

'Why did you leave?'

Maria knew this was coming. The Captain was a frequent visitor to Rare View and had a daughter her age.

'Telling Theodora I had to return to Italy was the only way to get her back to reality. And I was exhausted.'

She looked at the wall, waiting for him to make the final mark. He hovered over the smooth surface as though readying a depth charge. She struck the nail. They stood back to admire the five precisely aligned charts.

'What do you think?' the Captain asked.

'They're beautiful.'

She sat down on a straight-backed chair.

'There's a lot on your mind.'

'She's trying to buy that place – in Florence. The art historian's . . .'

'Jack Berman. I met Jack many times. We always got on well. You know what Thea said? That we were complete opposites – me and Jack. He didn't have a care in the world. It was a kind of genius he had. I could never do that – be like that. Navy discipline, I suppose. Is Thea really serious about that place in Florence?'

'The whole building is for sale. Someone already put in an offer. But she offered more, and has made a big deposit. She's asked them for a few more weeks because she doesn't have the money – the cash, I mean. Everything is in stock.'

'What's her plan?'

'She's taken on an investor. A client called Lewis Peters. He's closed some big real estate deal. I met him a few times.

I told Theodora I don't trust him. He's bought into the business. And she's moving the gallery to 76th Street. It's a good area – but a smaller space. All this will get her the property in Florence.'

'To live where Jack lived.'

'Yes.'

'But without Jack.'

'I think this man – Peters – is interested in her.'

'She's using him?'

Maria avoided the question.

'Maybe she'll move the company over there. There's space on the lower floors of the palazzo.'

The Captain stared at the charts on the other side of the wide salon.

'Seems like they've been there forever.'

'It means you have a good eye,' said Maria. 'That's what Theodora says when something is in the right place.'

'You know, when my wife died I went back to her favourite pictures over at the Met. One of them was ours – we donated it. But it didn't work. Going back.'

'Theodora doesn't want to lose.'

'She's a formidable woman. She got you to return. But—'

'She'll do anything to get that place back.'

Maria's voice faded with the evening light outside the gallery window.

'You avoided Mr Peters at Rare View,' said Kenji. 'The day he came in the helicopter.'

She was silent. During his early days at Rare View such moments made Kenji uneasy. Now they brought them closer. Then Maria took control again.

'She's keeping you here.'

'What do you mean?'

'She changed her mind. About Tokyo. It would take too long to set up. We'll take the exhibition over there for a few months instead. We can sell to Japan from here – you're already doing that. And we can add some business trips.'

'When did she decide?'

'A few days ago. Things have been unsettled recently – the company needs some stability. That's what Theodora says. She doesn't always tell people her plans – her real plans.'

'Not even you?'

'Not even me. In fact, I'm not sure she ever wanted to open a gallery in Tokyo.'

There was a pause.

'You are happy to stay with us, Kenji?'

'Yes, I am.'

When Appel called him to her office at Rare View a few days later, Kenji wondered if she'd say something about the reversal of her decision. As she rose from her desk he was sure she'd asked Maria to tell him.

'I'd like you to come to Italy with us. It'll help our preparations for the New York exhibition.'

'My visa is—'

'Don't worry about that. Maria has arranged your ticket. We're leaving the day after tomorrow.'

Kenji thought anxiously about his expired visa – it could be discovered on his return.

'I want to show you something,' said Appel, taking the tissue from the perfectly restored photograph. It was Jack Berman at the observatory in Florence. With a gesture that seemed both trusting and invasive she held it out. He took the photograph with both hands and bowed so low over it that she was looking at the top of his head.

'He asked me to move over there – four years ago. That's my biggest regret. The biggest regret of my life. Until then I don't think I'd made a serious mistake.'

He stared motionless at the photograph until she took it back.

'Work here a while,' she said. 'I've made some notes for the exhibition. Let me know what you think.'

He sat on the edge of the chair, not yet touching any of the papers on her desk. When he looked up she was gone.

It was late when Kenji left Rare View. As he approached the front door of the guest house, he saw the man in a gabardine overcoat sitting on the sofa inside. Kenji hesitated at the window, then opened the front door. The man didn't get up. It was the former employee who sold the stolen maps back to Appel.

'Kenji, isn't it?' he said earnestly.

'Yes. Good to see you again, Scott.'

The older man noticed the puzzled look on Kenji's face.

'I'm staying here a while. Theodora wanted someone to keep an eye on the place while you're all in Italy. I'll take the room at the back, if that's all right.'

'Yes, of course. Would you like something – coffee?'

'No thanks. I was in Alexandria just now.'

He got up and walked towards the atrium. He'd lost weight since their first meeting.

'It's nice here now. But freezing in winter. I stayed here when I first started with the company.'

'Yes, it's very cold in winter,' said Kenji.

'You like it here? In America, I mean.'

'Yes, very much. Ms Appel is a very—'

'She knows – doesn't she?'

'Excuse me?'

'She knows about those maps. The maps I sold her.'

He turned back towards the living area, knowing Kenji wouldn't answer.

'She only let me stay because I knew Jack. Because we can mention him from time to time. I like Theodora. The way she keeps the door open – that's everything in business. We spoke on the phone. I had to ask for a favour – another favour. I've been paying down some debts. Need some time to get back on my feet.'

'You can use anything here,' said Kenji, opening a kitchen cabinet. 'There's a lot of food. I only found out about the Italian trip today.'

'Jack was a character – we used to go drinking together in DC. He used to coach Theodora with her public speaking. She was a regular at the Garden Club of America – all over the country. It's a great way to find new clients. She told me she's stopped all that.'

'I didn't know she was a public speaker,' said Kenji.

'I saw the helicopter at Rare View.'

'That was Mr Peters.'

'I know. He came on the auction scene a few years ago – just when I was setting up on my own. That's the other reason I'm here – to warn Theodora.'

I X

Esteemed Professor:

Greetings from America. I hope that you and Mrs Kobayashi are very well. I received your translation of Emily Dickinson's poetry this morning. I have read the first five poems with tremendous pleasure. You have rendered them exquisitely in our language. I doubt that I will have any suggestions – but I will write as soon as I have carefully read them all. I apologise now for the delay.

Ms Appel – who speaks very fondly of you – will depart for Italy tomorrow. She has asked me to accompany her. What you said in New York is true – she is radiant. Everything here revolves around her. She plays many roles, but she keeps her distance. Her house here in Alexandria is an open house. Ms Appel's disposition towards each person is what makes this place unique. At first I thought her world was fixed and immutable. But I have learned in these months that Ms Appel attaches great importance to another place: the home of her late fiancé, an eminent American art historian who lived in Florence. We are going there to view an exhibition of great maps at the Medici Library. This is part of our preparation for an exhibition of our own in New York. For this, I suggested the same theme as the exhibition you saw in Tokyo: Progress in Cartography. I thought this would be even more appropriate in America. But I was very mistaken. Ms Appel has a sophisticated view of such things. She sent me on a tour of great map collections so I could learn more. To her, maps are embedded in time. Their richness can never be lost – even though their world has passed away. I feel a great sense of responsibility because the New York exhibition was my suggestion. At first Ms Appel did not seem enthusiastic. But now she believes it will be important for the company. I hope to resolve the contradictions with my proposal while we are in Florence. We will be accompanied by another colleague, Ms Manetti, who is Ms Appel's personal assistant. I have learned much from this brilliant person.

I will read the draft translations while I am in Florence, and will write to you as soon as possible. Thank you for the postcard of old Tokyo. I placed it on Ms Appel's desk today and I know that she will be happy to receive it.

With sincere best wishes,
Kenji

X

THEY ARRIVED ON A breezy June day: the feast of John the Baptist, patron saint of Florence. A billowing fleur-de-lis banner was carried into the cathedral at the head of an ecclesiastical procession. Heralds in renaissance costume followed behind. Kenji let go of Maria's calm commentary and stared up at the group of life-size statues above the south doors of the octagonal Baptistery. An executioner's sword was drawn back like a racquet. A man kneeled in prayer. A woman raised a hand in horror. For an instant Kenji felt as though the bronze figures were in motion and that he, Appel and Maria were frozen in time.

They stayed at a villa hotel on a hillside south of the city. A pony and a goat – more like pets than farm animals – grazed at the high end of an olive grove. Maria said the ancient path was lined with purple irises in spring. She once stayed here with her father. The original features of the villa were gradually being restored – the owner was building an atrium with drapes and a heating system for canaries. He wasn't sure the birds would survive this far north in winter but the villa did have canaries long ago. He had read about them in a book. Wooden beams and red tiles showed an elegant thrift that Maria said was typical of Florence. From his room at the back of the villa Kenji looked down at three lily ponds that reminded him of the carp farm near his home in Mito. At dusk they met in the terrace garden – the scorched golden grass like an overused tennis court. A waiter escorted them to one of the circular tables and poured three flutes of prosecco.

'What shall we toast?' asked Maria.

'You toast, Kenji,' said Appel.

'Happiness,' he said.

'*La felicità*,' said Maria.

There was a note of surprise in Appel's voice as she raised her glass. 'To happiness.'

The panorama behind her and the perfect glow on her face made Kenji realise – as though given a second chance to meet her for the first time – that Theodora Appel was a beautiful woman.

'Are we the same here?' she asked. 'Maria, are you the same in Italy as you are in America?'

'In America I think in English. During the day at least. Are you the same, Theodora?'

'Jack used to say I was more receptive in Florence – more time to listen. I think that's true.'

'And you, Kenji?' Maria asked. 'Are you the same in America as you are in Japan?'

'Yes,' he said. 'I am the same.'

The fading light absorbed the darkness around Appel's eyes. The rhythm of cicadas was loud but soothing. Just after ten, an explosion lit the eastern sky.

'*I fuochi*,' said the waiter. '*Solennità del Patrono*.'

'Fireworks for John the Baptist,' said Maria. 'Patron saint of Florence.'

For half an hour they watched the virtuoso display that ended with a trinity of white bursts. Afterwards, as he wrote down the times and details of what he'd seen in his notebook, Kenji wondered if Maria had synchronised their arrival with this ancient itinerary.

In the morning Appel took them down to the city she'd first seen as a young graduate. She showed them the olive-coloured *audioguida* systems in the churches and civic buildings. Photo slides of celebrated works were framed in small glass screens. These light boxes were new when she first came to Italy – now they seemed antique. She remembered how proprietorial her friends from the language school had been. In their code the river was the 'Arnaux' – it sounded sophisticated. In Piazzale Michelangelo there was another *audioguida* box, perched preposterously at the famous panorama. Normally the recordings offered an audio caption for a single artwork or building. But here — with all of Florence below — what could be said in a few moments? The hot handset had no mouthpiece. Small red lights in an oblique map were synchronised with the main points of commentary. The clipped accent echoed Petrarch: 'This is Florence. This is the pearl of cities.'

Leaving the piazza they went up to the basilica of San Miniato and sat in the coolness of the crypt. In the monastery shop Appel bought a jar of honey and a small bottle of propolis. In the afternoon the two women went back to the villa. Kenji bought a sunglass clip for his spectacles and wandered the streets in his two-piece charcoal suit. Vendors at the central market greeted him in fragments of English and Japanese. In the fourteenth-century cloister at the side of Santa Croce, Henry Moore's Warrior raised a bronze shield with a resigned dignity — the left arm severed in some battle. Kenji passed through the portico of the Pazzi Chapel and looked into the serene grey-and-white interior that reminded him of the Room of Purity in the samurai lodge in Mito. In the fading light he stopped at the Arno and listened to the water rushing over the weir.

The next morning Appel and Kenji went to the San Lorenzo cloister for information about the map exhibition. Maria had an appointment with a dealer.

'Look – that's the orange tree I told you about,' said Appel. 'It's still here.'

She sat on the stone ledge. In the upper cloister there were young voices and the tinkle of empty glasses.

'They delivered the invitations this morning,' said Kenji. 'The reception is tonight.'

Appel wasn't listening.

'I'm fit in an old-fashioned way. That's what he used to say. It was here I first heard his voice. "Would you like an orange?" That was his introduction. He wore a blue blazer and a burgundy tie. We sat here – heads in the shade, hands in the sun – just like now. It's so easy to remember in a place like this.'

A door banged in the upper cloister. The voices and empty glasses were silent.

'Oranges are the fruit of the Medici,' he said, nodding towards the tree in the centre of the San Lorenzo cloister. He took a flyer from his pocket. 'And if you come to this, I'll offer you a glass of wine.'

He handed her the programme of art history lectures.

'I'm only interested in maps,' she said.

He paused with surprise.

'I have a map. Only one – but it's really extraordinary. An original. I'd like your opinion.' He held out his hand. 'Jack Berman.'

From the top of the stairs Theodora Appel heard music beyond an open doorway: Vivaldi – maybe Monteverdi. The salon was lined with wooden cinema seats. On the terrace table, flasks of red and white wine stood under a flapping parasol in the evening light.

'I didn't think you'd come,' he said, waving away the note in her hand. 'But could you do me a favour?' She frowned and smiled as he lowered his voice. 'Take the admission – it's not good for the speaker to be seen handling cash. And could you work the projector?'

People came up the stairs in twos and threes, some alone. Even in those early moments her perspective was shifting from guest to something else. The first image on the screen surprised her – an elderly woman scrutinising vegetables in the Sant'Ambrogio market.

'What is Florence?' the speaker asked, his accent now subtly changed, reminding her of a radio announcer from her childhood. He nodded from the shadows and she pressed the control – a picture of the diving board at the Bellariva pool. The audience laughed at the antics of children in the foreground.

'City of humanism,' he said, turning. But she'd already triggered the next: Cimabue's thirteenth-century *Madonna Enthroned*.

Afterwards some of the audience lingered on the terrace listening to his anecdotes about the city. When she made to leave he came over and said, 'You've forgotten my map.'

'I presumed it didn't exist.'

'It exists. A protected treasure.'

He opened the door of a cluttered bedroom. A free-standing lamp cast an amber glow on the sixteenth-century ceiling.

'What—' Appel whispered.

'The world as it was.'

The cloister was quiet. It was hard to believe there was such a peaceful place in the heart of the city. The sun was fiercer then, she thought. She had more stamina now. Her brow was dry – a small victory against time. The bells of the cathedral began to sound. She glanced at his watch on her wrist and felt a flicker of hope.

XI

APPEL DIDN'T GO TO the opening reception. The following morning she returned to the cloister with Maria and Kenji. They took the strangely proportioned stairway up to the Medicea Laurenziana Library where a man at the admission desk said they were the first visitors of the first full day. Beyond a brace of blackened globes, atlases in goatskin bindings were propped on reading stands. The maps were laid in walnut vitrines. Kenji drew a floor-plan of the conjoining rooms and made notes about the lighting and humidistats. A twelfth-century T-O world map was drawn in fine biro-like hand. This was the dominant medieval paradigm. Semi-circular Asia floated like a dome above the horizon of the T. Jerusalem was at the intersection. The lower left was Europe, the lower right was Africa. The left transept of the T was the River Don, the right was the Nile. Christ in Majesty was painted at the top.

'Paradise is always in the East,' said Appel.

'From Eden to Judgement,' said Maria. 'The whole of the world and the whole of time.'

They examined a vividly coloured *Geografia di Tolomeo*, open at a map of north-western Europe. Revisions of Ptolemy's *Cosmographia* gradually replaced the medieval T-O ideograms.

'Old prototypes were kept for as long as possible,' said Appel. 'Even when it became impossible to reconcile them with new discoveries.'

Kenji realised that was also true in Japan. 'The eighth-century Gyogi prototype was used for centuries after new surveys were made.' As soon as he said this, Kenji wrote it down beside one of the floorplans in his notebook. He recalled Maria's observation during the argument in the new gallery: that maps show the richness of their time. He was still searching for a new theme – but now he felt less anxious.

A section of the exhibition was devoted to Paolo dal Pozzo Toscanelli – a Florentine who corresponded with Columbus about a westward route to Asia. Maria read sing-song from a manual of sailing directions in Venetian verse. Benedetto Bordone's Ciampagu – a woodblock map of Japan from 1528 – showed a fortified port, an unnamed town and a mountainous interior. This was centred in a page of speculative text – a *geographia conjecturalis* – describing a place no European had ever seen. On a Spanish vellum chart, revisions were carefully painted over obsolete text.

'In Italian,' Maria said, 'we call them *pentimenti*.'

'Humanism—' Appel began.

'Better than enlightenment!' said Maria – theatrically quoting something Appel taught her long ago. Kenji followed behind as their laughter rang around the galleries high above the cloister and the orange tree. He felt ashamed of trying to advance his theme of progress by stealth.

After the exhibition they took a taxi to Settignano just outside the city. In the village café, pensioners laughed loudly as a child dragged a metallic chair across the stone floor. The simple decor reminded Kenji of Appel's disdain for ostentatious opening nights and the gossip of dealers at antiques shows. They had lunch on the narrow terrace overlooking a panorama of gently sloping hills.

'That space was perfect,' said Maria.

'The AT&T will be difficult – we need something to break up the space,' said Appel. 'Not just partitions – some kind of feature.' She turned to Kenji. 'Did you find those glass maps?'

'I'm still waiting for an answer from Wisconsin. Many objects from the American Geographical Society were sent there when they moved.'

'Try the Craft Museum – they might know something.'

'We could make a model of the dome in San Lorenzo,' said Kenji, holding out a postcard of the painted constellations decorating the sacristy vault. 'I can ask the carpenters who worked on the new gallery.'

'We don't have much time,' said Appel. 'This exhibition is to promote the business – to get people into the New York gallery.' She looked at the postcard of the celestial dome, turned it over and wrote down an address. 'Let's meet here for dinner. It's a special place.'

In the afternoon Kenji went to the Roman amphitheatre in Fiesole. The two women took a bus back to Florence. On either side of the shelterless country road, bulging walls held back the sloping rows of olive trees, reminding Kenji of the orchards in Mito. But the grass was longer than in Japan and the trees were twisted in unfamiliar shapes. Terracotta Madonnas, adorned with bright plastic flowers, stood in shaded niches. In Fiesole he stopped at a bar and drank cold sparkling wine before going into the amphitheatre. A black wooden stage was set over the ancient floor in preparation for an opera. He lay down, thinking about the treasures of San Lorenzo and the words of Appel and Maria.

When he woke something had changed. Two continents of cloud coursed swiftly across the blue sky. A warm breeze blew into the amphitheatre and out over the ancient forum. He shivered lightly and remembered the day on the Pacific coast when he was burned by the sun. His lips were dry and his hair was tossed as he sat up, staring at a small gecko on the ancient stone. The voices that woke him were fading towards the exit and an attendant was calling out. A young woman laughed as she ran towards the gate. A man followed with exaggerated strides. In the distance, the city was merging with the wine hills. Kenji took out the constellation postcard and clasped it in his hand.

He was an hour late when he rang the bell on Via Santo Spirito. Only at that moment did he wonder whose home it was. Austere grilles on the ground-floor windows were covered in thick dust. He smoothed his jacket as he walked up the darkened stairway, passing heavy doors, some of them boarded. The only light was from somewhere at the top of the building. The door was open. He heard Appel speaking rapidly on the phone.

'I don't see the problem. Hang them left to right! Plate order. It's as simple as that.'

There were two steps down to an open living area with red tiles. A rustic dining table, dark with age, was set for three. Appel continued with urgency.

'Ignore them! That's what you do. That's how we create value.'

Maria came out from the kitchen and handed Kenji a glass of white wine.

'Is this the professor's home?' he whispered.

'Yes,' said Maria. 'You should have seen it before. There were so many things – books, drawings, photographs, records – he loved music. I'll show you the terrace.'

A hose snaked between empty terracotta pots. There were fresh flowers on the marble table.

'That's the cathedral bell tower,' said Maria. 'It's Giotto's design – completed after he died.'

'This view is beautiful,' said Kenji.

Appel came through the French doors. 'You're here.'

'Sorry I'm late. I was in Fiesole and—'

'We're all late.'

She looked out over the city, taking a moment to come back from the phone call.

'It needs a lot of work – this place. On hot evenings we used to have the lectures out here. Those cracks up there – Jack used to joke about them – like they were part of paintings he showed. They loved that. My first visit was in June 1965. It was the year before the great Arno flood. The year the Vinland map controversy began.'

'That map was called the fake of the century at the Italian Geographical Congress,' said Maria.

Kenji thought back to his visit to Yale. He regretted not asking to see the Vinland map.

'The Mayor of New York and a Pennsylvania Supreme Court justice joined in,' said Appel. 'The arguments among chemists who tested it were as sharp as those among historians.'

At dinner they talked about the Hereford map – soon to go on display at the British Library. Appel told them the Mappa Mundi Company had failed to raise the minimum subscription. 'Peters was right about that – less than a thousand shares were taken up. The locals are still trying to block the auction.'

After dinner, as Kenji smoked at the far end of the terrace, he half heard the two women murmuring about another time in this place – about Jack Berman's lecture cycle, about a congressman who took refuge here from the press, about the endless heat that was a bond with the past.

'We'll stay here for the rest of the trip,' said Appel. 'The owners are renting until it's sold. And it'll be more central for your research. You can move in tomorrow.'

They gazed at the view for a moment, then returned inside.

'Shall I close—'

'No,' said Appel. 'I'm staying here.'

Kenji and Maria took a taxi back to the villa. The patio furniture was stacked neatly to one side and the waiters had gone home. The sky was thick and a warm breeze swirled around the garden. A long salmon curtain, half caught in a balcony door, moved slowly in the breeze. They walked through a gazebo with climbing roses and down the steps to the botanical garden. Maria leaned in to read the tags.

'Blue Star. Silver Queen. Prinz Heinrich Anemone. These names are wonderful.' Behind a high hedgerow there was a trickle of water in a narrow stream. 'Atmosphere,' she said.

'What do you mean?'

'Atmosphere – Theodora always says how important it is. For clients. How Rare View has a special atmosphere.'

'Has it changed?' asked Kenji.

'Yes, it has changed. That's what she wants here. The atmosphere of what's gone.'

'What was she like before?'

'She was more fixed on people. It was always business – but she had an intense interest in people. You could see it by the way she looked at them. Now she doesn't have the same time for conversation. Theodora always made time – she was happy.'

'Like in the photograph?'

'The photograph?'

'In the magazine.'

'Yes. Like the photograph in the magazine. Everyone used to get an instant presentation on some great map. When she met new people in Washington she'd invite them down to Alexandria – sometimes after midnight. After Jack died that all stopped. Rare View is quieter now. She knows it'll never be the same.'

Maria led the way through a narrow channel of hedge and stopped before a delicate willow with luminous white bark, its branches cascading like fireworks.

'It's not good for her to be down there – on her own, I mean.'

'It will be better tomorrow,' said Kenji. 'When we go.'

'Florence isn't good for her. But I can't—'

'You can't say that.'

'Whatever she's planning – that's what she will do. I'm afraid—'

'What?'

'I'm afraid for her. She hides things well. But it's her grief. It's distorting her judgement.'

They looked down at the city as though waiting for the silent panorama to reveal something. In the city palazzo Theodora Appel sat by the marble table for another hour, then she walked slowly through the darkened salon, along the empty passageway and into Jack Berman's room.

XII

MARIA TYPED INTRODUCTORY LETTERS on an old Olivetti, signed them with Appel's name and gave them to Kenji with directions to the Biblioteca Nazionale and other collections in the city. After several visits to the science museum he was allowed to use the small reference library off the entrance hall. He spent hours on each paragraph of his exhibition proposal – frequently trying to recall the paragraph he gave Appel for her letter to Maria – as though remembering his own words would inspire him now. He carefully transcribed the captions of illustrations in catalogues and cartographic histories. Sometimes he took these to the Japanese assistant he met in the Peruzzi leather shop where he bought a pair of shoes on his second day. She was happy to translate for him. When she was busy he waited outside a framing workshop further along the street, watching craftsmen smoothing ornate frames with blackened fingers.

Even in the sharply delineated shade, Florence was hot

and humid. Kenji had no appetite and tried to remind himself to eat at fixed times, but this timetable was soon abandoned. In the afternoons he sorted his notes in a small café by the Arno. The owner told him, in halting English, that it was renovated after the 1966 flood. He pointed to the ceiling, still marked with circular scars. The furniture had surged with the water, etching the strange swirls into the plaster. The walls had been repainted but the ceiling wounds had been proudly preserved. In Kenji's exhibition dossier there were sections on conflicting astronomical systems, vanishing points in renaissance panoramas and controversies about the New World. He knew all this was too convoluted for the exhibition. 'The maps shouldn't be in chronological order – or by cartographer,' Maria told him. 'You can't force their meaning – that's what we saw at the Medici Library.'

While in Florence, Maria also told Kenji more about Appel's relationship with the art historian. At Rare View she only recounted anecdotes about the business – but here she spoke in a more preoccupied way – as though trying to better understand Appel's state of mind.

After their first meeting Jack Berman began an amusing but insistent transatlantic correspondence with Theodora Appel, who was ten years his junior. Their relationship blossomed that winter. His schedule was Florence from March to November and America for the winter months.

Five years before moving to Italy, he'd started a PhD on representations of commerce in Renaissance art. It was a mix of art history and economic history that would later become topical. 'Research ahead of its time,' he often joked. Although a brilliant undergraduate, Berman didn't have the patience for years of dedicated research. As meetings with his doctoral supervisor at Columbia University became less frequent, his field trips to Italy grew longer. When his funding ran out, he considered becoming a tour guide but abandoned this because certification was complex and lengthy. He taught English for three months, until a professor who needed help with a conference presentation told him: 'You should be giving this lecture.' With money running out, Berman distributed photostat announcements with details of a cycle of art history lectures. He was stunned when thirty cash-paying patrons arrived the first evening. Afterwards he spontaneously offered to take four perplexed German women to Paszkowski's – one of the most expensive cafés in the city.

The lectures took place in his apartment on Via della Spada, not far from the train station. But after complaints about noise from the family downstairs, Berman rented a bigger apartment on Via Santo Spirito. Here he installed old cinema seats in the broad salon. In the hottest months he beamed his well-rehearsed slideshows onto the wall of the adjacent building. An interval for wine was subsidised by the restaurant along the street which he recommended to visitors. Berman became popular among local art historians. They liked his informal status – far removed from their own factionalised academic scene. He translated scholarly papers and, in the early years, published some articles himself – diligently sending these to his now-retired doctoral supervisor. But as the lecture cycle became more successful he limited himself to short items for the *Philadelphia Inquirer* about art thefts, controversial attributions and the exhumation of renaissance bones. This was the man who introduced himself to Theodora Appel in the cloister of San Lorenzo in the summer of 1965, Maria told Kenji.

During their first winter together, Appel and Berman lived in a partially furnished Washington sub-let. She was starting her map business, he was collecting reference books and slides to expand the lecture cycle. At the start of the season he returned to Italy. Appel joined him for August. In November the following year, the Arno burst its banks and flooded Florence. Appel joined a group of volunteers who came to clean the mud-soaked city. The night she arrived Berman proposed to her. She didn't say no – the question was deferred.

Their only rift came eight years after they met. It was one of his throwaway remarks – part of the running commentary that made him a gifted public speaker. 'Come on, Thea,' he said, 'time for your business persona.' They were getting out of a taxi in front of the Dutch ambassador's residence, a few days before Berman was due to leave for Italy. It was a work appointment for Appel – the ambassador was a discerning collector. Berman was already showing their invitations to the guard. But Appel was standing where the taxi dropped her. He realised it was serious when he glanced around.

'I meant it like "It's showtime" or "Time to rumble" – something like that.'

But Appel's expression was vacant and betrayed. She knew there was no malice. He'd said something that Appel thought true. At dinner her voice was flat and she didn't press the ambassador to visit Rare View. When they left there were taxis outside but she preferred to walk in the early spring air. When Berman returned to Italy he sent her one of his amusing postcards – Maria once showed Kenji the shoebox archive of these beside Appel's desk at Rare View. When Appel didn't reply, Berman flew back to America. He arrived at Rare View after midnight, paid the taxi driver and asked him to wait.

'You never know.'

'The lights are on,' the driver said helpfully.

'The lights are always on,' said Berman.

He rang the bell. Appel opened the heavy door and smiled. From that night their relationship continued as before. Kenji tried to imagine this man wandering the galleries and offices. Maria said she remembered him most by his sudden laughter and the loud music from the apartment above. Appel heard the news at the Winter Antiques Show.

A secretary from the New York gallery told her Berman had been taken to hospital.

'Theodora just turned to me and said, "You're in charge here,"' Maria told Kenji. 'Then she left – I didn't see her for three months.'

Jack Berman was buried near his childhood home in suburban Philadelphia. Maria told Kenji what Appel told her.

'After the funeral, I stood with his relatives and a few others – maybe fifteen of them. I wish his Italian friends could have been there. The people who came weren't close to Jack. The talk was too brisk. After an hour I drove to the places we knew – Valley Forge, the Merion Cricket Club. I parked the car in Villanova and walked along an unfinished section of interstate. You know what it's called? The Blue Route. It's been held up for years. Jack loved that place. He used to say a road without traffic is especially peaceful. I walked until it was dark. Then I packed an overnight case and flew to Italy.'

It was only the second time Theodora Appel had seen Florence in winter. When she got out of the taxi she suddenly recalled how cold the city could be. There was music from the subterranean restaurant on Via Santo Spirito. A woman in an apron began to cry when Appel came in. Her husband solemnly brought out the keys.

'I'm very sorry, Miss Theodora,' he said. 'Everybody loved Professor Jack.'

They walked along the street in silence. He unlocked the palazzo door. She looked up at the grey steps.

'Would you come up with me?'

'Of course,' he said softly. 'I have to turn on the electricity upstairs.'

The windows were shuttered, the apartment in total darkness. The flame of his cigarette lighter threw their shadows around the open salon. He flicked a switch, then another. The overheated lighter went out. Appel, who was moving cautiously towards the terrace doors, was plunged into darkness. She remembered the two steps down to the open living area. Even in daylight Jack warned guests about these. She could hear his voice now. She held on for a moment. The restaurateur found the switch and the bulbs flickered. The wooden cinema seats were covered with white sheets. Appel went to a free-standing lamp and turned it on. The light was soft. She turned off the ceiling lights and opened the French doors. He stood at her shoulder looking out at the panorama.

'It's beautiful,' he said, as though he hadn't noticed his city for a long time.

'Yes,' she said, half expecting the beauty etched in the clear winter night to have gone. She stood there for a moment. He touched her arm. He must have asked something. She tried to smile and said, 'I'm fine.'

'Are you sure?'

'Thank you. It's all right. I'll come for lunch tomorrow.'

He smiled and frowned, knowing she wouldn't.

'Please come by, Miss Theodora.' He left a card on the table and turned towards the door. 'You have the keys?'

'Yes—'

Her voice choked as he turned away, his shoulders hunched against her cries from the deserted terrace.

XIII

THE WOODEN SHUTTERS WERE closed against the searing July heat until Maria opened them at dusk and the rooms filled with an orange glow. When she left to visit her family in Lombardy the apartment remained in darkness. Kenji saw Appel less frequently – she rose early and he usually returned after dark. Sometimes he had the impression she wasn't there. The stack of research notes grew steadily on the wicker table in the corner of his room. When he had a morning appointment he stayed up through the night drinking sparkling wine, or the Talisker whisky he found in the kitchen. He noticed that the map of Scotland on the label was not the same as the map on the presentation carton. Sometimes, in the middle of the night, he walked softly along the passageway with empty bookshelves and out onto the terrace to smoke a cigarette by the marble table.

In the Museo Storico Topografico he studied plans and prospects of Florence displayed beside a model of the ancient Roman town. In the Palazzo Vecchio he examined the great wall atlas painted by Egnazio Danti and Stefano Bonsignori with cartouche texts in gold lettering. A giant globe – like some ancestor of the anniversary globe he saw at the National Geographic Society in Washington – stood in the centre of the great atlas room. It was stiflingly hot. A single fan turned slowly beside the custodian's chair. He photographed Egnazio Danti's panel of the coast of Asia with 'Giapan' lying in the rich blue ocean. Danti also designed the Vatican Map Gallery and worked with the papal commission on calendar reform. Space and time were also inseparable in Japan. Globius's father was an astronomer who worked on calendar reform for the Shogun. Kenji learned that Egnazio Danti conducted astronomical experiments at the Dominican basilica, so he went to the facade to examine the quadrant for measuring the height of the sun. But it was almost dark and a lamp mounted high on the Grand Hotel Minerva was distorting the shadow. He resolved to return the next day.

But an alternative research agenda was forming in Kenji's mind. Instead of going back to the astronomical instruments, he stopped at the Loggia dei Lanzi to look at Cellini's statue of Perseus holding the severed head of Medusa. A few paces away were copies of Michelangelo's *David* and Donatello's *Judith and Holofernes*. He lit a cigarette and let the spray from the fountain of Neptune fall lightly on his hair. At the kiosk on the other side of the piazza he flipped through the metallic racks and bought a monochrome postcard of a headless statue on a plinth beside the Arno. A man at the historical archives said it was the statue of Primavera at the north end of the Santa Trinita bridge. He showed Kenji a pre-war photograph with weeds sprouting from the arches and Primavera with her right arm swung high. On the night of their retreat in August 1944, German troops detonated the bridge to slow the Allied advance. The archivist showed him another photograph – an iron Bailey bridge strung across the stumps of ancient stone. After the war the bridge was meticulously rebuilt and the statues restored. The motto of the effort was *Dov'era e com'era*: Where it was and as it was. But the head of Primavera couldn't be found. The headless statue was remounted on the plinth. Multilingual notices were sent around the world by Agenzia Parker Italiana on the assumption that a soldier had taken it as a trophy. The pen company offered a reward of $3,000. In 1961 the head was found during excavations on the riverbank. Kenji approached the restored statue in the brilliant sunlight. Primavera was swathed in a chaotic gown, her left breast bare and one foot lightly raised. The right arm was lost but the left balanced a basket at the hip. There was a fine line where the head had been reattached.

In the austere hallway of the Istituto Geografico Militare an officer in green uniform told Kenji he needed special permission to use the map library. Kenji presented Maria's letter and the officer took it upstairs. When he returned he told Kenji the letter was not sufficient – the introduction would have to come from the Japanese army. Kenji laughed out loud but quickly stopped because the spontaneous cackle sounded more mad than mirthful.

After dark he walked through the city as cleaners swept the streets and whining trucks emptied septic tanks. He passed heavy doors left slightly ajar, inviting a draught in the stifling heat with an ancient, even sinister confidence. Kenji remembered how Appel once described Rare View as a renaissance palazzo – visitors were welcome day and night. Sometimes he sat on a bench in the Frescobaldi garden opposite the apartment. One night he fell asleep there for a few hours, and dreamt about the plum garden in Mito, the homeless angels high above the Park Avenue Armory, the samurai lodge and the sparks flying into the gloaming. In the nocturnal living room mosquitoes played at his temples as he struggled to concentrate. He mixed the myths of Florence with the story of the Shogun's astronomer, Globius, and his own disoriented belief in progress. He read his professor's translations of Emily Dickinson's poetry and wrote him a letter suggesting three changes. He felt tremors in the earth that reminded him of home. He wrote to his mother, describing Florence as a city of temples – like Kyoto – and asking her to post his school atlas to Rare View. He thought again of the day long ago in the school infirmary. The silence between them about this, he thought, was perfect love.

When his letter from Italy would arrive, his mother would read it to his father while he ate. He would show no obvious sign of interest – itself a sign of great interest. He would not read it – he never did. His mother's calm interpretation of everything would be right. 'Really?' he would say over and over as she relayed the contents. And each time the word 'really' would convey a different sound and sense. It was a whole language generated from one word: sometimes a murmur, sometimes a question, sometimes a fascinated guttural note, sometimes a suppressed laugh, sometimes a tone that wondered if something were wrong.

At night Kenji sprinkled the terrace tiles under his bare feet while watering the potted plants. He heard summer thunder rumble loud and dry. When the storm finally broke he was at the high end of the Poggio Imperiale. He walked along the earthen path in the imperfect shelter of cypress trees – his charcoal suit and open white shirt soaked with summer rain. His new shoes were strangely comforting. He'd spent the afternoon at the observatory library where – instead of preparing for the New York exhibition – he'd been side-tracked by an exhibition of photographs and maps from a 1913 expedition to central Asia. As Kenji approached the river he noticed a strange multi-coloured reflection on the low storm clouds. On the Ponte alla Carraia he looked west along the water. The south bank was bathed in red light, the north in blue. A line of white bulbs was strung across the diagonal weir. He walked along the bank. A small crowd had gathered outside the Institut Français de Florence. There was a National Geographic poster of bicentenary fireworks exploding over the Eiffel Tower. A laughing girl handed him a rain-soaked brochure explaining the *mapparilievo* – a relief map in bronze by Mario Mariotti. This was the prototype for the vast installation of lights along the river Theodora Appel called the Arnaux. But it was not until Kenji stood at the centre of the Amerigo Vespucci bridge that he understood the awful whole. The parallel quays of the Arno were its sides. The diagonal weir, strung with lights, was the giant bicentennial blade. The geography of the river was fashioned as a guillotine.

During his last week in Italy Kenji collapsed. That morning a woman at the science museum said something about books he'd requested from storage. Kenji half remembered a missed appointment. He apologised, reordered the books and set out for the geography reading room at the university. But he felt weak and went into the church of San Giovannino to sit down. Then he felt a twitching sensation in his foot. He opened his eyes – as though waking for the first time that day. For an instant he thought of an appointment at the science museum. His cheek was resting on the smooth floor. Fluid shapes swam in the corners of his vision as he propped himself on one elbow, perspiring and nauseous. A woman said something in another language. Kenji repeated the word 'taxi' and she hurried to the sacristy. He didn't remember falling. He touched his unbroken teeth. There was blood on his forehead.

When the taxi arrived at the villa driveway, Kenji realised he'd given the wrong address. The concierge recognised him from the night of the fireworks. Together they explained to the driver that he needed to go to Via Santo Spirito. Kenji walked slowly up the steps and unlocked the door. As he passed the salon someone came in from the terrace. He didn't turn as he heard Maria's voice.

'I think there's something wrong with Theodora.'

Kenji moved along the darkened passageway, his open hand on the empty bookshelf. He stopped abruptly when he saw Appel standing by the desk in his room. Even though the shutters were closed against the fierce sunlight, he raised his hand to cover the congealing blood.

'Progressing?' she asked.

'I'm writing it up now.'

'That portrait I told you about in New York was sold for thirty-five million. The Halberdier – by Pontormo. It was painted here in Florence. It's a record for an old master picture. You got there just in time.'

Kenji was silent.

'Are you all right?'

He half turned, catching her image in the speckled mirror. 'Just tired.'

'They tested the fidelity of a sixteenth-century telescope

here this week,' Appel said. 'It's almost as good as a modern instrument.'

He was afraid she would notice the blood on his forehead. But the room was dark.

'Did you hear anything last night?'

'No. Nothing in particular.'

'Around eight?'

'No, perhaps I was out.'

'The doorbell rang – just before eight. The audio isn't working – but I knew what it was. The same thing happened a few nights ago and I opened the door. It was a couple. They'd been to one of Jack's lectures five years ago. They were wondering if he was here. They were from Minnesota. I invited them up – told them what happened. We had a glass of wine on the terrace. I thought it was wonderful how they remembered – how they came back. The bell rang again last night. It must happen a lot. I didn't answer.'

When she left, Kenji pulled off his clothes, soaked with perspiration. He lay motionless, staring at the white ceiling, suddenly thinking of his plan to restore a telescope to the roof garden in Tokyo. All was silent in the stifling heat as he closed his eyes. Then he remembered Maria's words.

'I think there's something wrong with Theodora.'

XIV

'STRANGE THINGS HAPPEN IN Florence,' said Maria. 'My father says people become obsessed here. And you never eat.'

For a while she said nothing. Kenji woke with a jolt. It must have been the silence she shaped in the shuttered room.

'Have some of this,' she said, pointing to a dish of cold *soba*. 'The Japanese girl at the leather shop had the noodles. I found her number on the table.'

'She translated while you were away,' said Kenji. 'For the exhibition.'

'She speaks very good Italian. I thought you'd like some Japanese food.'

'How did you find out?'

'There was blood on your shirt.'

'Did Theodora—'

'Theodora's gone to Venice. There's a conference on seventeenth-century astronomy.'

'She told me she wasn't going.'

'I know. That's what she said. But someone came over from America.'

'You said there was something wrong.'

'She's better now,' said Maria. 'It was a bad day – for all of us. We argued. I told Thea I don't understand what she's doing. She wouldn't explain. She told me to focus on the New York exhibition.'

'I have to finish the plan,' he said.

'We have more time now.'

He closed his eyes again.

'That night – in New York – why did you come back to the new gallery?'

'Why are you asking that now?'

'I was just thinking—'

'I was worried about you.'

'About me?'

'You need to look after yourself, Kenji. Eat this – you'll feel better.'

The next day Kenji returned to the hill of Fiesole to work on his notes. It was hot but there was a firm breeze. In the afternoon he felt strong enough to walk back to the city along the steep rustic lanes. At the church of Fonte Lucente a plaque said the water flowing through the niche was good for the eyes. He splashed some onto his face and washed away the last trace of the scar on his forehead. Further down the hill he saw two peacocks moving silently across the gravel of a villa forecourt. In the centre of Florence he stopped to look at the Baptistery again. He'd read that the octagonal shape of the building evoked the eighth day – eternity beyond the rhythm of earthly time. High above the south doors he studied the bronze ensemble he'd seen during his first moments in the city. The recoiling figure, an oval plate under her left arm, was Salome. The executioner's sword was raised. The kneeling man was John the Baptist, patron saint of Florence. His hands, protruding from the line of the facade, were joined in prayer. The marble beneath him was streaked with four centuries of slow green copper.

'*Mare agitato*,' said the ticket lady at San Zaccaria. There would be no boats for two hours. The water was too rough – the wind blowing into Venice almost a gale. It was a relief to be away from the pressure of Florence. Theodora Appel walked out to the edge of the deserted wooden dock. The green water slapped hard against the swaying timber and the moored gondolas. A girl on the fourth-floor balcony of the Londra Palace looked out over the lagoon and sang the opening lines of a song in German. This was a good moment – not a moment she had chosen, but one imposed by the delay. She opened her purse and took out the pack of cigarettes.

Just after three, the vaporetto started out across the

basin. Appel had been to the Lido before. Jack Berman took her to the film festival the year *Gloria* shared the top prize with *Atlantic City*. It was there she bought the Murano chandelier for her New York gallery. She took a taxi to the Adriatic side of the island. The waves were topped with white surf beneath two layers of horizontal sky – a light blue and a darker, almost wintry, indigo. The green domes of the Hotel Excelsior came into view – the name in blue-and-gold mosaic. She was two hours late. The concierge complimented her on her Italian, but spoke in English as he came out from behind the desk.

'Yes, madam – this way please.'

The terrace was deserted, except for the figure at the last table. Tame sparrows flittered to and fro between the potted palms and the white railing. Lewis Peters rose to greet her. He was dressed in a long cotton shirt with a small towel at the back of his neck. His forehead was sunburnt.

'Don't worry,' he said when she apologised. 'I'm having a perfectly enjoyable time.'

Lunch had been cleared away but a glass of wine remained. Appel was surprised when Klara called Florence to say Peters was in Italy. He had seen her name on the Venice conference list in the *Map Collector*.

'You're looking well, Theodora.'

'Italy is wonderful.'

'Let's have something to drink.' He beckoned a white-jacketed waiter. 'A Scotch and—'

'Coffee, please.'

'Americano, madam?'

'No, espresso. Thank you.'

Their conversation was convivial until Peters asked how long she planned to stay.

'I'm going back to Florence tonight—'

'But the conference!'

'We always sign up for those kinds of things. It's good for the company – gets our name around.'

'You mean you're not—'

'No. I don't have the time.'

'But there's a dinner – some big people over from New York.'

'I can see those people any time. My priority is to prepare for the exhibition.'

Appel sensed that Peters's patience, for whatever he wanted, was beginning to fade. And, for the first time, she doubted whether she could keep up the facade that obscured her own deception.

'You're not losing interest, are you, Theodora? I mean – a lot of important people will be there.'

'A lot of important people come to me. To my company. I don't need to chase them.'

The waiter set a silver tray on the table. Peters raised his glass towards Appel. 'And how are we doing?' he asked.

She knew what he meant, but stuck to her theme.

'The preparations are going well. We're studying the

exhibition in Florence in great detail. It's given us good ideas for the layout in New York. The Italians are the best at this kind of thing.'

'I mean – how are we doing with our stock?'

She took up the cup and spoke slowly.

'We're in Italy to prepare for our exhibition in New York. These preparations are essential for the business – and for capitalising on your investment. If it's done right, the exhibition will generate a lot of footfall through the New York gallery – and a lot of sales.'

She felt a flicker of satisfaction, knowing he was unused to being addressed so directly.

'And, after five months, I wouldn't mind some return soon.'

'This is the art market. It takes time. As I told you – art outperformed stocks by seven points last year. But art is sensitive to price. Value is not the same as liquidity.'

She lit a cigarette.

'I didn't know you smoked.'

'I do – sometimes,' she said, fixing her gaze on the row of beach cabanas. Maybe it was the flapping canvas or the scent of the cigarette that brought it back. The midnight walk along the beach after a screening at the film festival. Jack wearing a tuxedo and she a black jacket and straight black slacks. Her uniform, he called it. She once scolded him for that word. Now, as she peered along the beach, she longed to hear it again. How far had they gone before he took off his shoes? How far before they lay down on the sand?

'How's Maria?' asked Peters.

'She's with me – in Florence. We're making plans. After the New York exhibition we're taking everything to Tokyo. That's why I hired Kenji – the young Japanese man. The market is booming over there.'

He was looking at her intently, now admiring her acumen. But the cigarette in her steady hand increased his belief that she was hiding something.

'I brought this from Florence,' she continued, placing the exhibition catalogue on the table.

He picked it up.

'I'll let you know if I have time to come down to Florence. See it for myself.'

It was these words that made Appel profoundly uneasy as she walked back along the Excelsior terrace. Peters's presence in Florence would be a violation – something against nature. Perhaps this was what caused the incident with Maria when she got back to the palazzo that night.

Kenji witnessed this from the salon. Appel and Maria were standing at the end of the passageway. There was a strange lack of energy in the dimly lit scene. Appel took the company camera from Maria.

'I got quite a shock when you showed up here that spring,' said Appel. 'You do realise that?'

Kenji stepped away.

'We were worried about you,' said Maria. 'I left the company to get you home.'

'Home?' She smiled wistfully. 'It worked. The business would have collapsed with both of us over here.'

'Yes,' said Maria, her voice a dry whisper.

'It was very mature of you, Maria. It was a reversal – to draw me out. To remind me there are other people in the world.'

Appel carefully turned the camera in her hands.

'But I had to come back to Florence. He was dead over there. There was still something here.'

She opened the camera case.

'I remember one morning – soon after I came over. There was a strange yellow glow. I looked out at the rain. I thought it was my eyes until I saw a woman on the next terrace staring across the rooftops. She saw it too. When I went out, the cars on the street were smudged. Sand from Africa, they told me – carried on the wind. It's called *l'effetto Sahara*. The sand comes down with the rain. There were tiny contours of sand in the streets.'

Appel released the sprocket and with a swift motion extended the film in a black arc. There were about ten exposures.

'We have enough pictures of it at Rare View.'

*

The next evening Kenji realised what Maria was photographing. He finished the exhibition proposal and went to Appel's room. Through the open door, a free-standing lamp cast an orange glow on the restored photograph of Jack Berman in a simple walnut frame. He knocked, but Appel wasn't there. He set his dossier of text and photographs on the sideboard. An ant crawled across an unopened jar of honey. Appel's passport lay on a thick stack of hundred-dollar bills. Kenji suddenly thought of his overstayed visa. He meant to speak to Appel again. But since the day Maria told him something was wrong, he knew he'd have to do this on his own. He moved closer to the photograph. The line of the repaired tear was barely visible. As he turned to leave, his eye was drawn up to the coloured ceiling. Even in the dim room, the aquamarine sea and verdant Italian plains were clear and vibrant. Kenji recognised this as the map in the photograph he'd seen by Appel's desk on his first day at Rare View. This was the place. Kenji was so astonished by its precision and beauty that he momentarily took off his spectacles. Gazing up at the vaulted fresco, he shuffled gently so as not to trip. This was the centre of Appel's universe – the renaissance world of the man she loved. And for this place, with its map and unfinished compass rose, she was risking everything.

'Beautiful, isn't it?'

The words so startled him that it took a moment to register Maria's voice. He put on his spectacles.

'The world as it was,' she said. Now he understood.

He took a step forward. She was already there, reaching out to touch the scar on his forehead. Their surprised lips took a moment to penetrate. Their eyes closed and the room around them fell away.

Lewis Peters sat alone on the Excelsior terrace in Venice. Half an hour after Theodora Appel had left, a waiter asked if he would like another drink. Peters declined with a shake of his head. His expression was heavy now, his lips pursed. He reflected on how much everything had changed. While waiting at the hotel he had felt a surge of hope as he thought of meeting Theodora. He allowed himself to savour some perfect confluence of his business and personal life. What went wrong? Was it simply the weather – that she was late? He recognised the pattern: high hopes, some kind of misreading of the situation, a dissonant note, a sense that he needed to protect himself. Why couldn't people see things his way? Why was this so complicated? He was successful – and generous. He tried to dispel a sense of anger. The waiter came back with a piece of paper.

'Put it on my room.'

'Sir – it's a message from the front desk.'

Peters opened the typed note. There was a man waiting for him in the lobby. Peters had told him not to approach, in case he were still with Appel.

'Bring him out.'

The man, who was about forty, wore a grey tracksuit.

'What kind of place is it?' asked Peters, without salutation.

'I haven't been able to get inside. But it's impressive — austere — a sort of palace. Five storeys high. Looks like it could do with some work — but it's solid.'

'How did you find it?'

'It was easier than I thought. Berman's still in the city phone directory.'

The sun had set on the other side of the island — but there was a warm afterglow.

'Will I go back to Florence?'

'No. Go back to New York. I'll take care of this myself.'

The day before they left Kenji found his unmarked exhibition draft on the living-room table. He couldn't tell if Appel had read it or not. At the post office he mailed a box with his alternative research to Rare View. Maria joined him in the afternoon and they bought a case of Castello di Verrazzano and a folio guest book from Pineider for the New York exhibition opening. Maria took him to see the astronomical sundial in the cathedral. As a schoolgirl she'd sat along the gradations in the floor listening to a guide explain the quest for the solstice and Easter Day. She told Kenji how the windows in the octagonal lantern above the dome were covered on Midsummer's Day – except for a single pane to project a sunbeam across the meridian in the marble floor. They returned to the basilica of San Miniato which they'd visited with Appel. To the right of the choir they saw the full-length portrait of Saint Miniatus surrounded by an eight-panel narrative. The first Christian martyr of Florence died during Emperor Decius's suppression in AD 250. The panels showed him arrested, then calming a leopard set against him, then miraculously surviving a furnace, a primitive rack and boiling oil. In the penultimate panel, Miniatus kneels before an executioner raising a sword. In the final frame Miniatus staggers up the steep Florentine hill miraculously clasping his severed head.

On the way down to the city, Kenji and Maria stopped at Piazzale Michelangelo and played the *audioguida* recording again. Kenji was surprised how much Italian he could under-stand. At the Ponte Santa Trinita, headlight beams flashed on the white statues of the seasons. Bats flew up from the buttresses of the faithfully reconstructed bridge.

'You're thinking of her,' said Kenji.

'Yes. I'm thinking of her.'

'Curtis said it's not a company at all.'

'Did he say that?' Maria asked with a smile. 'He's partly right. For people who work in New York it's fairly normal. For us – well, you know what it's like for us.'

Kenji realised she meant they lived and worked for Theodora, not the business.

'How did she find you?'

'Jack Berman recommended me after an interview on the terrace. It seems so long ago.'

'They brought us together,' said Kenji.

'Theodora and Jack.'

'You called it the place of the past.'

Maria paused. 'I did.'

'Maybe now there's something else.'

'A future?'

'You don't regret what happened – in that room?'

Maria didn't answer. Then she leaned in and kissed him.

Lewis Peters got off the train in Florence in the early afternoon. It was hotter than Venice. He wore sunglasses, a blue linen suit and a white shirt. It was his first visit to the city. He walked to the Grand Hotel on the river. The balcony overlooked the Arno. It was a spectacular southern panorama. But it raised in Peters a feeling of resentment. It was the same resentment he felt when he used to visit his former in-laws in Massachusetts. He had planned to go straight out again, perhaps to see the map exhibition in San Lorenzo, because he wanted to be able to discuss this with Appel. That was the plan at breakfast time. To surprise her. To confront her, but reasonably. They were partners, after all. And he couldn't be sure – he still hoped – that his suspicions were unfounded. Now, as he closed the heavy curtain on the view and lay on the bed in his jacket, he felt the need to find out as much as possible and, if necessary, get out of the partnership. Why was it that they would not respect him? He was a cultivated man – always learning. And yet he struggled with people like this. They seemed cannier, even though they were worth less. He closed his eyes. He replayed the conversation in Venice. She was tough, and it made her more attractive. He wanted to believe it was an act – like her bravado with the designer at the Winter Show. That had been for him, he knew it instantly. He was a businessman, after all – one of the best in New York. Had he blinded himself to her stratagem? What was her stratagem? He relaxed his shoulders in his tight jacket and dismissed the idea that she was going to make some kind of escape with the money. Why had he thought such a thing? He was cautious in business – some said paranoid. He knew they said this. His wife's lawyers had said it – and had written it down.

He woke with a jolt. The room was cold. He got up fully dressed and switched off the air conditioning. He opened the window. He felt better now. He showered, combed his hair straight back with gel and changed his shirt. He would go to Appel's apartment. They needed to talk. He would be reasonable and everything would be cleared up. A huge sum of money had changed hands. He just wanted to be sure his investment was safe. He checked the map again for directions. Via Santo Spirito was just across the river. He had a cocktail at the hotel bar. Then he went out, crossed the Ponte alla Carraia and turned left into Via Santo Spirito. He calculated that the palazzo would be no more than fifty yards on the left side. Suddenly he saw her step out and pull the heavy door. Appel wore a white cotton dress with a suede jacket draped on her shoulders. She turned left – he was now ten paces behind her. He caught the word 'Theodora' at the top of his throat. His eyes narrowed. For no reason, he glanced behind him. Was this what people did when they were following someone? She walked ahead at an even pace, her auburn hair swaying between her shoulders. Her head, as always, was high. She didn't pause or glance at the windows on the street. He held back as though some moment of action had passed. Then he relaxed. He would follow her and when he was ready, he would speak. He settled into a steady stride about twenty paces behind. She turned left onto the Ponte Vecchio. It was crowded with dinnertime tourists. He moved closer. Appel turned right off the bridge and within two minutes, turned into the stairway of the rowing club. Peters passed the open door but didn't look inside.

Appel was saving this for her last evening in Florence. In the drab dining area beneath the great galleries two couples played cards. She was ready to show his membership card, but nobody checked. Canoes and mooring booms swayed in the slow water by the riverside restaurant. Red and white roses grew along the bank and thick ivy crawled the wall. Low sunlight beamed through the arches of the bridge. The waiter escorted her to a table on the lawn. With one artful motion he swept away the setting opposite and asked if she'd like some water. She answered in Italian and – as soon as he'd turned away – the man at the next table complimented her.

'Ah – you have an advantage over us.'

His wife pointed to a phrase book between two dessert plates. 'We get by with this.'

'I only know a little Italian,' said Appel. 'I really—'

'It sounds wonderful,' said the man, slurring his words.

'Are you from America?' asked his wife.

'Yes – near Washington.'

'We live in Vancouver. The organisers of Alex's conference gave us a guest pass. This place is so wonderful.'

'Yes,' said Appel. 'Is it a good conference?'

'Don't ask.' The man laughed. 'It's about compressors.'

For an instant Appel felt a small shock – his age and voice reminded her of Jack.

'Florence is quite famous for science, you know,' she said softly.

'We love Florence,' said the woman. 'Are you on holiday?'

The waiter brought her a carafe of water and put two liqueurs on the adjacent table. Appel ordered red wine.

'Not really – I'm tidying up some things.'

She frowned as she thumbed her glass, sensing the man was about to probe.

'See this river? When I was a student – it's a long time ago – we used to call it the Arnaux.'

Lewis Peters looked down from the balustrade. Hanging plants obscured the diners. He turned back to the bridge, crossed to the other side of the river and stopped opposite the rowing club. Appel was seated alone in the busy bankside restaurant. Peters went to a café and had a panino. Then he had an idea. He would go back to Via Santo Spirito and ring the bell. He could tell Maria or the Japanese man that he was in town. Maybe he could get to see the apartment. He walked briskly along Via Santo Spirito and stopped at the high door. Beside the top bell there was a faded brass plate with the name *J. Berman*. Nobody answered.

The soft bulbs in the hanging garden dimmed before midnight and the conversation of diners was replaced by the murmur of staff. The voices from the balustrade above were softer now. Appel ordered coffee, lit another cigarette and paid. The breeze carried voices from the other side of the river. Long after midnight she walked carefully to the heavy green door at the slipway. It was locked. She looked

quizzically along the deserted garden. How long had it been?
She pulled the jacket around her shoulders even though
there was no chill. She heard her own small laugh as though
someone she loved were listening. When Jack first took her
to this place they hid along the bank until dawn. Now it was
an accident, a door closed, someone forgotten. She appreci-
ated the logic of this oversight. It wouldn't have happened
if she had been with him. If she were whole. The waiters
would have heard their voices. She touched his membership
card in her pocket. How many hours before the starlings
announced the dawn?

Lewis Peters was incredulous as he saw the last two waiters
pull the slipway doors behind them. Theodora Appel was
seated in the shadows about forty yards to the left, calmly
smoking a cigarette. They'd forgotten her. He thought of
running over the bridge and calling out to the waiters. But
this would cause a commotion – and she would know that
she'd been followed. Then he felt an uneasy sensation. Perhaps she had seen him. Surely this wasn't possible – he was
just a silhouette across the Arno, among the picture-takers
and lovers. He watched her uneasily. There was a calmness
in her posture. Just after two o'clock he turned and went
back to the hotel.

*

Kenji and Maria walked to the edge of the medieval centre, crossed the wide boulevard and passed the old train station. Traffic sped by the outdoor pizzeria beneath a giant plane tree. Potted plants were covered with the thick dust of the summer road. Taxi drivers parked and ordered coffee. Girls stood at high tables. Nobody seemed to pay. On the other side of the avenue, tour buses were parked outside modern hotels. From behind a neon sign reading *Central Park* there was the throb of an outdoor nightclub. A green laser traced a strange and delicate line across the Florentine sky. As he looked upward Kenji remembered straining to see the painted starry vault of Grand Central Terminal in what seemed like an older world.

At dawn they turned towards Santa Maria Novella. The sharp light of morning showed Egnazio Danti's four-hundred-year-old timepieces in perfect order; the quadrant on the right of the facade, the armillary on the left. They stepped into the porch of the basilica that the scientist used as a great camera obscura. Then they saw her. Theodora Appel was sitting in a custodian's chair, sobbing. Maria rushed to her, threw her arms around her neck and kissed her.

XV

THERE WAS A THUNDERSTORM at Kennedy airport. Kenji took his old Japanese business card from an Italian cigarette pack. He was anxious now – sure they'd catch the overstayed visa. Then he changed his mind. He wouldn't present his department store card. He crumpled it in his fist and dropped it on the marble floor. This small gesture brought him a sense of calm. The immigration officer looked at his passport and asked him to wait. Moments later a colleague arrived and escorted him to an office with white soundproofed walls. For an instant Kenji thought his tranquil demeanour might make him look ill. He consciously sat erect and blinked his eyes.

'When were you last in the United States?' the supervisor asked in an almost deferential way.

'I was here in June.'

'And for how long were you here?'

'From January to June.'

'And what were you doing?'

'I am organising an exhibition.'

The supervisor looked at Kenji's passport.

'Your visa was for ninety days.'

'I'm sorry. It is taking more time than I thought.'

'What's your position, sir?'

'I'm an art consultant – at a gallery.'

'Do you have some documentation on that?' the supervisor asked.

Kenji handed him the exhibition dossier with the address of the AT&T Tower and the September opening date pencilled on the cover. As the supervisor flicked through notes, photostats and floorplans of the Medici Library, Kenji was glad he'd posted his strange alternative research directly to Rare View. He wouldn't have been able to reconcile it now. The man left with the portfolio. There was no sound. Maria and Appel had taken an earlier flight from Milan. They would be at Rare View by now. In the silence of the small room Kenji tried to envisage the Momiji tree at the end of the lawn – it would have changed colour while he was in Italy. The supervisor returned.

'All right, Mr Tanabe – there are no further extensions. It's sixty days. Next time you'll need to renew in Tokyo. I caution you: do not overstay again.'

Kenji felt relief and something like shame as he stood up.

'Thank you. It will be ready by then.'

They walked back to the hall. The desk officer stamped his passport. 'Welcome to America.'

It was dark when the taxi pulled into the Rare View driveway. The shrubbery beyond the cypress trees was thicker now and the grass was overgrown, making the property seem almost pastoral. Kenji took off his shoes in the silent hall. A desk lamp cast a homely glow through a gallery doorway. He left three copies of the Florence exhibition catalogue on Klara's desk and picked up his mail, which included two padded envelopes from Japan. The first – his school atlas – was still wrapped in the cover his mother made when he was a boy. The scent of the pages made it seem as old as the atlases he'd seen in Italy. Before this school book he would always be small. He needed to compare the section on historical maps with his selection for the New York exhibition. The school atlas had pictures of a terracotta map from Babylon, a map of the world based on Ptolemy's coordinates, a Japanese Gyogi prototype map, a T-O map with paradise in the East, a portolan chart of the Mediterranean, the Behaim globe of 1492, Blaeu's 1648 world map, Hachijo island from Tadataka Ino's great survey of Japan and a modern map from the Ministry of Construction. Finally he had made this succinct survey his own. Another envelope bore the insignia of Waseda University. He guessed what it was – his professor's translation of Emily Dickinson's poetry. But Kenji was stunned by the image on the cover – a photograph of the Kairaku-en gardens in Mito – his home town. Kenji suggested this in jest during dinner with the professor in New York, because the poet was a passionate gardener. For the first time he felt a darting, surprising desire for home. There was a letter from a curator at the American Craft Museum; she had no information about the stained-glass maps Kenji wanted for the exhibition. Another from the University of Wisconsin was also negative. The university, a leader in cartographic history, had accepted some artefacts from the American Geographical Society when it moved from Harlem to Wall Street. But not the Tiffany era glass maps.

From the hallway Kenji noticed that the blinking green cursor of the Lanier word processor was strangely reflected around the darkened library. His hand touched cold plastic where the bookshelves should have been. He found the switch and for an instant was dazzled by the glare on his spectacles. As he looked into the library the cold sensation came back to his ear – as though he were hearing the voice of his Tokyo director again. Around the room, the pages of the dismembered Ortelius atlas were mounted in protective mylar and pinned to the edges of the bookshelves. Kenji stepped forward and listened – not to any sound, but to the tension in the newly enclosed space. Beforehand, every noise was absorbed by the deep wooden stacks. Now, even his own breathing was audible.

The frontispiece portrait of Abraham Ortelius was at the

centre of the ensemble. The other leaves were mounted in plate order around the library. Brochures with terms of the offer lay neatly on the map chests. The breaking of atlases was not illegal but to Kenji it was deeply distasteful. The syndication was first suggested by Lewis Peters when he came to Rare View – the day Appel was pretending to have bought the great atlas with his investment. Kenji moved slowly around the library, horrified at the explosion of colour and form. The prospectus described the syndication as an opportunity to acquire a selection of maps from the English edition of one of the finest mapbooks ever made. The text must have been prepared with Appel's guidance. He suddenly remembered what she said on the phone in Florence: 'Hang them left to right! Plate order.'

Under the terms of the offer, each of twenty subscribers would get eight leaves of the separated atlas. The order of selection would be determined by lots, reversing through eight rounds. There were 160 leaves including the section on classical geography. Not included were the title page, preliminaries and a three-page obituary of Ortelius, who died eight years before the publication of the English edition in 1606. According to the prospectus, the atlas was lacking the map of Scandia in northern Europe. Kenji couldn't recall the collation of the great book, but he felt betrayed by the implication that it had been incomplete. He thought of taking down the 1968 facsimile to see if he could remember the Scandia map, but that volume was now sealed somewhere behind the leaves of the dismembered atlas. The prospectus described Abraham Ortelius as an innovative Flemish publisher and chart dealer. He was cosmographer to Philip II of Spain – his maps decorated the King's throne room. Rubens painted his portrait. The *Theatrum* was published in Shakespeare's England. Ortelius was a renaissance man who corresponded with Dürer, Erasmus and Egnazio Danti – the Dominican friar whose scientific instruments and painted panel maps Kenji had seen in Florence. He glanced up from the prospectus. The deformed Rare View library was now a grotesque imitation of that monumental atlas room. Soon the leaves of the great book would be scattered. Theodora Appel was closer to regaining the ceiling map and the home where she fell in love with Jack Berman.

Kenji sat at his desk. The last books he used before leaving for Italy lay undisturbed: a Japanese–English dictionary and a booklet published by the New York Public Library for an exhibition of maps. Since the shelves were now sealed, he put these in the desk drawer beside the magnifying loupe and the flask of vintage Japanese sake he intended to give Theodora Appel on his first day at Rare View.

XVI

As HE APPROACHED THE front door at Rare View next morning Kenji heard the argument between Maria and the senior accountant. There was a message on the answering machine – Peters demanding cash for three of the rarest portolan charts. He was entitled to this under the terms of the agreement with Appel. Kenji stood in the short passageway to the library. The argument continued on the stairs.

'We need to stall him,' said the accountant. 'That kind of stock cannot be liquidated overnight. He needs to understand that this is not real estate.'

'We need to pay him. One confident payment,' said Maria. 'It's the only way to stop more demands.'

Kenji stood at the entrance to the library. The leaves of the hand-coloured atlas were strangely beautiful in the morning light – as though they'd been liberated. Maria and the accountant were shouting now. Then the front door opened.

'Maria's right.'

They looked over the banister. Appel had heard them. She moved up to the landing where Kenji first saw her in the brilliant light of January.

'Peters is in some kind of trouble. Maybe he's not the big shot he thought he was,' she said calmly. 'If we don't buy in he'll try to force us to dump stock. And you know the rule: we never dump stock because the market would collapse.'

The house was silent.

'We need to pay him. Use the New York account.'

'That won't cover it,' said the accountant tersely.

Appel's voice was cold as she turned back from the door of the apartment. 'Then get it in Washington.'

Kenji's obsession with the broken atlas yielded to alarm about the state of the company. Appel had raised more than seven million dollars – now she struggled to find a million. A few days later Kenji understood why. There was a pause on the line when he answered the phone. He waited for a distant voice – maybe from Japan. But the call was from Italy. A man asked to speak to Theodora Appel.

'I'm sorry – she is not here,' said Kenji. 'Can I help?'

'It's about the property,' said the man. 'The documents are ready now. How should we send them?'

'We'll arrange this with Federal Express – we have an account.'

Kenji wrote down the estate agent's address, then lingered for a moment exchanging pleasantries while gazing across at the faded photograph of the vaulted fresco map in the gilded frame. Appel described Rare View as a renaissance palazzo – now she owned a real one. Kenji wondered when she'd met the Florentine agent to discuss the details. Perhaps it was the day they moved out of the villa, or the day he collapsed and returned to find her standing by his desk. The memory of heat and drifting days clouded even a simple chronology. Florence was far away, but it loomed over everything at Rare View.

'Is she here?' asked the tentative voice.

It was Scott. Kenji hadn't seen him since he left for Italy, even though he'd heard him in the kitchen the night before.

'Hello, Scott. She's upstairs – in the accountants' office.'

Scott looked up at the ceiling, then nodded towards the intercom.

'Can you call her on that thing?'

Appel said he should come up. They sat on a sofa in the corridor outside her apartment.

'Everything all right, Scott?'

'Yes, Theodora. I wanted to thank you again. For helping – for the room and everything.'

'Don't mention it – stay as long as you like. Stay forever if you want.'

There was a long pause.

'Scott, you didn't come here just to say that. We've known each other too long.'

'It's about Peters – Lewis Peters. I heard some bad things

about him, Theodora. About the people he's in with – in New York.'

'I know all about it.'

'I mean—'

'I said I know, Scott.'

'He's dangerous, Theodora.'

'I know about Lewis Peters. And I don't care. He wanted to be a player – so we played. And when you play, there are risks. That's called business. That's called life.'

'It's the opposite, Theodora. I'm warning you about—'

'Don't bother, Scott. Look at me – do I look afraid?' She glared at him. 'Do I even look like I'm living?'

The next morning Kenji joined the Rare View staff in the lobby of the Shoreham Hotel in Washington. The salesmen, accountants and restorers were all assigned exaggerated titles for the annual strategy conference Appel insisted on each year. Kenji's obsolete badge – *Director, Appel Galleries, Tokyo* – was printed in italics below his name. Klara told him they were attending the conference to counter rumours about a crisis in the company. There were presentations on sales, client trust and long-term planning. Exercises were set at the end of each session. State your company mission in under fifty words. What are your greatest weaknesses with clients? How could you expand? Appel seemed enthusiastic – although Kenji couldn't believe she was learning anything new. At the closing dinner she told staff to sit at different tables – to collect as many business cards as possible.

The businessmen with Kenji were curious about the rare map business and – for a moment – he thought of telling them the story of the Shogun's astronomer. But instead he explained how maps revealed their age in watermarks and traces of verdigris. After dinner the lights were dimmed and a film clip of the first moon landing reflected on the faces of the participants. A voice from the podium spoke about motivation and goals. The reel was speckled and the sound muted from the number of times it had been screened. In the old-fashioned glow of astronauts walking on the moon, Kenji noticed Appel and Maria moving towards the exit. He realised the crisis was deepening.

Kenji resented the scent of cologne in the library at the Ortelius syndication the following afternoon. Staff from Rare View and New York were assigned to the businessmen, doctors and lobbyists who came to divide the great atlas. The map chests had been moved to one side – except for twenty drawers tagged with the names of subscribers. An unsold share was in Appel's name. The driveway was lined with cars – many with diplomatic licence plates. Appel introduced Kenji to a lawyer who bought a share at the New York gallery. She said the salesman who sold it was unable to attend. But Kenji already knew about this. Maria told him Curtis

Hahn had resigned while they were in Italy. Kenji guessed the lawyer was one of his clients. While they waited for the draw he showed this man the frontispiece introducing the maps of antiquity. Two figures were engraved on either side of the Latin title: a man holding a celestial globe and a woman holding the terrestrial. At the foot of the page was the maxim *Historiae Oculus Geographia*: Geography the Eye of History.

Appel moved among the clients, greeting them by name as she did at the Winter Antiques Show. Klara folded numbered lots and put them in a Montelupo fruit bowl. The interns brought out an elaborate board with the subscribers' names — the order reversing through each round. There was a cocktail atmosphere as clients, spouses and friends mingled in the library and the front gallery. Kenji observed from a corner — a prospectus rolled tightly in his hand. He was familiar with its contents by now. The syndication was an opportunity to own part of an historic portfolio. That's what the atlas had now become — a portfolio. The subscribers broke into applause when a man from the Whitney Museum wearing a green bow tie held up the number one. When the first round began he picked the world map — Typus Orbis Terrarum. The map of America was chosen second. The Maris Pacifici was third, followed by the famous map of Iceland surrounded by exotic sea life. Maria drew the unsold share for Appel. It was lot five, and she selected Japan. Since the eight maps would be returned to stock, Kenji knew she'd chosen by price. A three-panel map of Florida was taken by a businessman from West Palm Beach. Kenji's client was seventh. He picked a map centred on the East Indies, from the eastern tip of Arabia across to the western shore of America, with barrels from a wrecked galleon floating in the Pacific. Maria was assigned to advise a curator from the new National Museum of Women in the Arts. She drew lot fifteen. Kenji watched as the two women lingered by the plates of ancient geography – ignored by the other subscribers. Klara called out the plate number and an intern wrote it on the board. Clients gathered to look at the map of the Mediterranean, Europe, North Africa and part of Asia. Around this scheme was an empty, pumpkin-like graticule, confidently drawn for future discoveries in the regions of Frigida, Temperata and Torrida. Other subscribers moved cautiously across the room, for the first time considering the ancient perspectives.

When the order reversed, the collectors' interests became clearer. A doctor from the National Institutes of Health picked the map of Holland and an oval-bordered map of the Netherlands. In the second round Maria's client picked sixth. The other subscribers looked at the two women as though they possessed some unnerving knowledge. They selected the Paradise of Thessaly showing the wooded slopes of Mount Olympus and the Helicon flowing into the Aegean. Kenji's client picked Argonautica – a map of the central and eastern Mediterranean showing Jason's voyage. The man

from the Whitney and the woman from the National Museum
of Women in the Arts compared their maps of renaissance
and ancient worlds. Kenji examined the peach-coloured Isle
of Skye on the map of Scotland, remembering his nights
in Florence studying the Talisker whisky label and carton.

Slowly the leaves of the atlas were taken down and Kenji
saw the library books for the first time since leaving for
Italy. In a Smithsonian exhibition catalogue he showed the
lawyer an allegorical painting by Hoefnagel with Ortelius
shown as an owl. Appel once used it as a catalogue cover.
Kenji looked at the maps chosen by Maria's client. Along
with the grid for a world not yet known and the Paradise of
Thessaly, there were maps of the Azores, Bohemia, Namur
and the territories of Siena. Maria was also making Appel's
remaining selections. With two rounds remaining, Klara
beckoned Kenji towards Appel's office. He was about to enter
when a man sitting outside said, 'She's on the phone.' He
was about forty-five, dressed in a light grey suit and – in
contrast to the formally dressed guests in the library – no
tie. When Kenji introduced himself the man said, 'I used
to work here. It's Phil.'

'Pleased to meet you. I'm Kenji.'

Appel opened the door.

'Remember our friend from Louisville?' she asked.

'Yes – what about him?' asked Phil.

'He's getting married the day after tomorrow – in that
hotel.'

She held a beige folder with the words *Account stopped* on the cover. The man seemed to revert to a nervous gait that Kenji half recognised.

'Are you sure?'

'I found out a couple of days ago,' said Appel. 'Maria got an invitation.'

'Maria came back?'

'Yes,' said Appel curtly. 'I think this provides an opportunity to retrieve our property.'

Kenji thought back to the winter day when Appel bought the maps from Scott. Her tone was harder now. He listened, trying to catch unfamiliar names from another time at Rare View. The bridegroom in Louisville was also an ex-employee. After leaving the company he opened a hotel with two partners. A client told Appel about the stolen maps – which were used as collateral to finance the renovation.

'He's getting married in the function room. My maps are on the walls. I want them back. Or a cheque for six hundred thousand.'

'He'll listen to me,' said Phil. 'It's not as though he can run from his wedding without being noticed.'

He stopped grinning when Appel spoke.

'I remember. He was a pal of yours.'

She turned to Kenji.

'I need you to go to Kentucky. You can take turns driving. And could you bring in the new exhibition draft?'

As Kenji left they began to discuss the man's fee. A buffet

THOMAS BOURKE

was laid out in the main gallery across the hall. A small child
ran barefoot on the wooden boards. There was a burst of
laughter from the library. Maria was in the far corner, surrounded by clients. When Kenji returned to Appel's office the
man was gone. He handed her the draft exhibition catalogue.

'Should I go back to the client?'

'He'll get the hang of it – he's a lawyer,' she said. 'Sit
down.'

Appel turned the portfolio text and images. From across
the desk it was like a school project in her hands. In the
silence he realised this was the first time they'd sat facing
each other across the desk. Usually they stood.

'This is good,' she said. 'And the wooden dome is terrific.'

'Palmiro is painting the vault like San Lorenzo.'

'A map of the heavens. By the time we look up at the
stars, they've already changed. Like we're looking back into
the past. Did you like Florence, Kenji?'

'It's beautiful – very beautiful.'

'But do you like it? Could you live there?'

'I think I could—'

He stopped himself. He wanted to say something about
his visa. He wanted to say something about Maria. He
wondered if she knew about them. The two women shared
everything. But he couldn't tell.

'What about those glass maps?'

'I haven't found them,' Kenji replied. 'Nobody knows
where they are.'

'I'd like to see them.'

'I'll keep searching, but—'

'I know. I know.'

She held one of the map transparencies to the desk lamp. Her face was tired.

'Time,' she said softly.

In the hallway Kenji heard an intern call the eighth and final round. Evening sunlight streamed across the toppled books in the library. Subscribers cheerfully called out numbers in what was now a kind of parlour game. Kenji overheard the curator in the bow tie say to Maria: 'I've just realised – in this round I don't get to pick – I get the one left over.'

Appel clapped her hands and, without warning, introduced Kenji who would tell them about an important company event. He was never sure if such instructions were delivered abruptly because she thought he might demur – or because she instinctively trusted him. The subscribers fell silent as Kenji began to speak. Without hesitation, he listed the rarest maps by heart – more than ten – and offered one fact about each. He concluded by saying he hoped they would come to the opening at the AT&T on Madison Avenue. As they broke into impatient applause Kenji wondered if Appel's invitation for him to speak might be her apology for the broken mapbook of the world.

XVII

'SHE BETTER NOT BE setting me up,' said Phil, getting into the van. Kenji put away the road atlas and started the engine. His companion began to speculate in a tone of unconvincing menace.

'If these people refuse to talk we'll call the police – or threaten to call the police. That'll be your job. They'll listen to someone who works for the company.'

Kenji didn't say he was on a tourist visa with no extensions.

'If we get the maps, we'll cross into Indiana. I know these people – they'll say we stole them. We have to be very careful.'

Kenji drove slowly between the limousines in the Rare View driveway. Chauffeurs smoked in the lengthening shadows of the cypress trees. A warm breeze blew through the long grass.

'I suppose she told you about the fight,' said Phil.

'The fight?' asked Kenji.

'Why I left.'

'No,' said Kenji. 'She didn't.'

The man considered this by slowly nodding his head. When his voice came back, it was tinged not only with relief but with half-remembered wonder.

'This place – always something. There's something magical here.'

'Atmosphere,' said Kenji.

'It's impossible to replicate. I almost miss it. I do miss it. I remember – years ago – we spent a week trying to recreate the Rare View look in New York. We moved every stick of furniture. But it didn't work – it could never work – so we changed it all back again. I hear there's a new gallery now.'

'At 76th and Madison,' said Kenji. 'It's smaller than the old one.'

'She keeps in touch with us, you know – the old staff.' Phil laughed to himself. 'Not because she loves us! It's for information. That's the most precious thing in the market. You know what she calls us? The ghosts.'

'The ghosts?'

'She calls us the ghosts. That's what I felt like back there just now. And one day, kid, you too will be a ghost.'

In Charleston they stopped for fuel and coffee, intending to find a motel soon after. But when the stranger beside him fell asleep, Kenji continued west through the night. He thought of the maps being dispersed in the library, of

Maria's encouraging smile as he explained the exhibition and of Theodora looking down from an upstairs window as the last of the visitors drove slowly away.

When they arrived at the hotel in Louisville, the door was opened by a porter with epaulettes and a top hat. Maps hung prominently in the consciously old-fashioned lobby. Kenji's companion phoned the bridegroom from the reception. He spoke without a word of introduction.

'We're downstairs. I'm here for your own good. You know what she can be like.'

Kenji suspected they'd already spoken by phone during the break in the journey. The bridegroom – overweight but neatly dressed in a black blazer – came down and glanced around the foyer.

'Is she here?'

'Not yet,' said Phil opening the dossier. 'I don't care how you got these maps – I'm taking them out of here right now.'

He pushed the list into Kenji's chest.

'Start ticking them off.'

The bridegroom moved closer.

'Most of them are in the suites – they're occupied.'

Phil looked up at the ceiling and shook his head.

'We need maps – or money. Otherwise she wants us to wreck your big day.'

'Still on commission, Phil,' said the groom.

'I didn't create this problem, pal.'

'How much does she want?'

They stayed in a suite on the third floor. Kenji phoned Rare View but Appel had left for a meeting in Washington.

'She sold the workshop this morning,' said Maria. 'Take whatever they offer. Peters wants his money. He knows something is going on – something about Florence.'

The bluntness of her words startled Kenji.

'I think he must have been in Florence – when we were there. After Thea met him in Venice. You better get some sleep – and get back here soon.'

'Maria—'

'Not now.'

A judge officiated at the wedding. Some of the guests recognised Phil and said how thoughtful he was to come such a long way. As the guests began to waltz, the bride-groom and Phil beckoned Kenji to join them. They were reminiscing about their days with the company.

'Appel stories! Let's have the latest!'

Kenji hesitated as he looked at their expectant faces. They poured him a glass of bourbon. He began cautiously, by telling them about the New York exhibition. But then something happened. He remembered her words: 'This business is about stories. Just make it up – that's what Maria does. Use me. That's what I'm here for.' Kenji told them the exhibition would travel the world. And it would leave new galleries in its wake. 'She's lining up financing from J. P. Morgan. We're going to create a network of client investors. A film producer found us a location off Rodeo Drive in Los Angeles. Our new Tokyo gallery will be the best in Japan. And we're setting up a gallery in Florence. That's why she got Maria back. That was the idea all along. From the start.'

The two men stared hard at him – riveted – with their drinks lowered. He couldn't stop. The phrases he'd memorised from her visits to the library tumbled out.

'She has an idea – a cycle of lectures about the history of science in the new gallery in Florence. There will be a roof terrace with telescopes. We're taking everything to a whole new level.'

They drank with abandon. The men chuckled with a mix of fascination and envy. Because they were ghosts, they had no alternative but to believe it all. They knew not to underestimate Theodora Appel – for whom anything seemed possible. She wanted her staff to be imaginative. That way, they could bring the maps to life – bring another time to life. That way they could sell. Kenji wove his fluid fantasy as an alternative future of the company. Perhaps it was his mastery of company facts, mixed with a lack of sleep and the surge of alcohol, that helped him weave a scenario so convincing that at some point in the evening he thought he might resolve everything. This dreamscape – this *conjectur-alis* – might boost the company beyond all danger. Above all, there would be happiness – what he toasted to on their first night in Florence.

Kenji woke in the back of the van in the hotel car park – a cheque for $500,000 in the pocket of his jacket. He didn't remember going to the van. But he must have preferred it to the hotel room, perhaps sensing some danger. His companion would fly back to Washington later in the day. As he started the engine Kenji had the notion to visit the Virginia estate where he left the Mediterranean chart retrieved in Pittsburgh. The yellow blossoms in the fields reminded him of the scattered broom of Tuscany. When he knocked on the white door the client came out in an oriental dressing gown. Kenji bowed deeply and hoarsely delivered the message he'd committed to memory.

'The company needs the chart for an exhibition in New York, sir. Can we have your decision, please?'

As the client peered at him, Kenji realised how strange he must have seemed – dressed for a wedding and unexpected. The man fumbled with the switch dangling behind the frame – the first time he'd used it. Together they gazed at the rare portolan chart. Wisps of blue cigarette smoke rose from the client's fingers in the draughtless room. For a silent instant, buoyed by the fantasies of the night before, Kenji's hopes soared. Then the man gave his answer.

'Son, you better take it to your exhibition.'

When Kenji arrived at Rare View, the staff meeting was ending.

'We need to raise cash,' said Appel. 'Contact your best clients. And we need to make sure the exhibition opening is a big success. Peters wants to dump his stake at auction but I'm stalling him with lawyers. If the exhibition opening generates enough sales, we might be able to keep him on board. If not, the auction will go ahead. That's all.'

Everyone left, except Maria.

'I can talk to the agent in Florence. You could put it back on the market. There would be capital gains, but my father has—'

'No,' said Appel in a tone that was both light and final. Maria had heard it many times – when a counter-offer was rejected or when she declined to take a client's call. Dealers called it her endgame voice.

Kenji worked to restore the library as it had been before he left for Italy. While workmen manoeuvred the walnut map chests back into place, he put the remnant atlas plates in a leather case: the frontispiece, the dedication, the three-page obituary of Abraham Ortelius, the introduction reprinted from the first Latin edition, a profile of the cartographer and the frontispiece with the words *Historiae Oculus Geographia*. Even though he should have been preparing for the New York exhibition, he worked late into the evening pulling the books out to the edges of the shelves and meticulously smoothing each row. When he came to the maroon-covered Ortelius facsimile he opened it at the reproduction of the Scandia plate – allegedly missing from the broken atlas. Even in this uncoloured copy it was a handsome map showing Russia, the Baltic, Islant and Groenlandt. He clearly remembered the original. The broken atlas had been complete.

Kenji spent hours looking for an illustration that could double as a cover for the exhibition catalogue and an invitation card. He finally chose an image from *The Light of Navigation* by Willem Janszoon Blaeu. The engraving, by David Vinckboons, showed a seventeenth-century master of navigation with scrolled charts, a compass and an hourglass. A harried group of novices fidgeted with instruments while the master pointed to a terrestrial globe with one hand and gestured for patience with the other. Although the figures appeared to be in an interior space, the architecture provided no apparent cover. In the background, ships were tossed on a choppy sea. Neptune and Aeolus stood in high alcoves at either side. The light of the title burned brightly above the group – it seemed neither day nor night. Kenji called a courier to take the artwork to a print shop in Washington. The Rare View library now looked the same as before – except for the broken Ortelius atlas. He opened the desk drawer, took out the ceramic flask of vintage Japanese sake and slipped it into his jacket pocket.

At the AT&T Tower on Madison Avenue the following afternoon, specialist art handlers moved the framed maps into the exhibition space. The electricians and carpenters who worked on the construction of the New York gallery greeted Kenji warmly. The Venetian chandelier from the old 57th Street gallery hung unlit in the shadows. When Maria arrived that evening, their embrace was spontaneous and anxious. They sat beside a full-scale model of the Parisian fountain dedicated to Marco Polo, *Explorateur de l'Asie*. On a pedestal festooned with fresh garlands, a gilded orb floated in the middle of a celestial scheme.

'Theodora told me about Louisville,' said Maria. 'You did very well. That was more money than we expected.'

'Did you know those people?'

'Yes. We worked together. I was surprised the cheque cleared.'

'I suppose she sent the money to Peters,' said Kenji.

Maria said nothing. The high industrial lamps cast a cold glow on the painted fountain – making the grey basin seem like real stone.

'We have to test this before the opening,' she said. 'It'll look better when the spotlights are on.'

'I saw the photographs of the original—'

'She sent it to Italy,' said Maria, stretching the pockets of her cardigan to her knees. 'The Louisville money. That was the last payment on the property. There was about fifty thousand left over. She's putting that into the exhibition.'

'But what about Peters?'

'She's obsessed with that place. She doesn't care about risk anymore. She's embracing it now.' Maria looked around the exhibition space. 'Strange how we are surrounded by maps and yet so lost.'

The next morning Kenji found a white envelope lying inside the gallery door. He knew it had been delivered by hand – it was too early for the daily bundle. It was addressed to Theodora Appel. He picked up an antique silver blade and opened it. Peters's Brooklyn address was printed at the top of the page. The typed note bore neither salutation nor signature. The auctioneers had been unable to guarantee the reserves on the principal lots. The estimates Appel assigned to Peters's stock were described as exaggerated beyond current prices. There would be no auction. Peters was demanding all his money – plus interest – immediately. His name was typed at the foot of the text. Kenji sat down at the reception desk and read the note again. Appel had few friends at the auction houses. She frequently told clients how they colluded on commissions. They didn't hesitate to challenge the high values she'd assigned to Peters's stock.

Above the hallway in Captain Bonne's Park Avenue apartment, cotton clouds were painted on a blue sky. The fresco was precise and realistic. But to Kenji it was strangely empty compared to the painted ceilings of Italy. In the darkened salon beyond an archway, the five charts installed by Maria were propped against a sofa. The Captain had agreed to lend them to the exhibition. The brass pinions of a pair of seventeenth-century Hondius globes sparkled in the early evening light. Between the high windows there was a huge d'Hondecoeter painting of peacocks in an ornate frame. The scent of an extinguished cigar hung in the homely air. When Kenji phoned that morning, the Captain agreed to meet him but couldn't fix a time. Occasionally a maid passed silently without acknowledging him. Kenji repeatedly checked his watch, thinking of the art correspondents he should be calling with reminders of the opening. He thought again of Appel's surreal calm when he phoned Rare View to read Peters's demands.

'Buyer's Remorse,' she said dismissively before he had finished reading. 'How's the exhibition progressing?'

'We still have some work. But it looks good.'

'Have they changed those lights?'

'Yes,' said Kenji. 'Maria looked after that. But shouldn't—'

'And my chandelier?'

'It works.'

'Good. That's important.'

'Do you want me to read the rest of the—'

'No, I don't,' she said. 'You focus on the exhibition. I'll see you at the opening.'

When Kenji told Maria about the letter they decided to approach Captain Bonne and Lewis Peters. It was only now – as Kenji sat in the silence of the Captain's apartment – that he wondered why Maria insisted on going to see Peters. It was Maria who hung the five charts in the Captain's apartment, and Kenji who last met Peters at the Rare View inventory lunch. Another hour passed before Captain Bonne arrived. Kenji thanked him for the five charts – a very valuable contribution to the exhibition. He then delivered his proposal. His mouth was dry, his words mumbled. He didn't believe his own proposal – it sounded as though it were coming from someone else in the shadows of the room. Appel had invited an investor – Mr Peters – to take a stake in the company. She then invested his stake – but Kenji didn't say how. Peters was now pressing to liquidate his investment. Appel bought in some of the maps but the company was unable to cash any more of Peters's investment. Kenji asked if the Captain would be interested in buying part of the portfolio. The company would sell this over time – repaying him with interest. 'It's a sort of loan,' he said quietly. Then he waited for an answer – one way or the other. When the Captain closed the spectacles Kenji hadn't noticed in his hands, he knew he'd failed. They talked for a few minutes. But later, when Kenji recounted this meeting to Maria, he couldn't recall what was said after the Captain made that small motion. He only remembered walking towards the door and shaking hands under the painted sky.

XVIII

Kenji was surprised that the only light in the new gallery was from the halogen bulbs above the maps. Maria hadn't returned. He checked the address on the note from Peters and drove to his house in Brooklyn Heights. As he approached the townhouse he heard their voices. Maria was at the top of the steps beside the open door. An imperial Roman torso loomed under a spotlight at the end of the hall. Peters, wearing a crisply ironed business shirt, was shouting incoherently. A man in a grey tracksuit stood behind him.

'It's over! Finished! And so are all of you!' he yelled as Maria edged back to the steps. The other man looked down with a tranquillised gaze. Maria stumbled as she turned. For an instant she seemed not to recognise Kenji. He gripped her arm – the crumpled note with Peters's address still in his hand.

'Do you have a car?' she asked, glancing back.

'Over there. What happened?'

Her lips were white but the words were businesslike. 'He knows about the building in Florence.'

Baseball players kicked up the summer dust in Central Park. A man cycled slowly, selling beer from a basket. Kenji and Maria joined the line of patrons by the outdoor theatre. It seemed right that their day somehow continue – even though they'd failed in their missions to Bonne and Peters. An executive at Hitachi, the sponsor, had sent complimentary tickets to Kenji with a note thanking him for invitations to the exhibition opening. The murmuring theatre-goers moved slowly in the evening glow. When they arrived at the amphitheatre the attendant said loudly, 'You don't need to stand in line – these tickets are VIP!' Patrons looked at them curiously and for a moment they felt like imposters. As they passed through, someone called out their names. Kenji almost didn't recognise Curtis, who now had long hair and was holding an infant.

'Great to see you two!'

'Hello, Curtis,' said Maria.

'This is Hattie. And our daughter, Coretta.'

'She's so beautiful,' said Maria. 'Congratulations!'

'Thank you,' they said together.

'What are you doing now?' Maria asked Curtis.

'Night classes – graphic design.'

'I remember you talking about that – your dream.'

'It was time. There's a lot of tension over there – in the new gallery. A lot of rumours. What are you going to do, Maria?'

She blushed – for an instant off guard.

'I'm happy with Theodora,' she said quickly.

'Say hello to her.'

'I will,' said Maria.

'I hear you're quite an expert now, Kenji. My orphaned lawyer was impressed.'

'We're preparing an exhibition at the AT&T Tower – maybe you can come to the opening,' said Kenji.

'I'd like to do that.'

'We'll leave an invitation at the door.'

The bell rang. Patrons hurried into the amphitheatre as the lights dimmed. Kenji and Maria took their seats with the Hitachi executives near the front of the stage. In the September breeze the Kabuki company chanted, strummed and mimed the story of Medea. At the interval Kenji explained the world of Kabuki. Maria laughed when he called the Shogun 'generalissimo' – the word used in old western histories of Japan.

'Do you think we're like them?' she asked him.

'Who?'

'The actors. Are we like actors?'

'Someone else in control?'

'Yes – someone else in control.'

After midnight they walked to the gallery and sat in

the shadows. Maria opened one of the bottles of Castello di Verrazzano they brought from Italy for the exhibition opening. A passing couple stopped to admire the window display.

'I love old maps,' said the man.

'They're beautiful,' said the woman. 'Let's come back.'

The voices faded. The gallery was as silent as when Kenji slept there during the renovation.

'Should we contact the company where she used to work?' he asked Maria. 'The brokerage.'

'I already did that. The man who started the corporate collection is retired. He went to Montana.'

She sat in the director's chair, beneath a poster of Saul Steinberg's 1976 *New Yorker* map in playful pastels: the wide expanse of 9th Avenue, then 10th, the Hudson, Jersey, Kansas City, Nebraska, the Pacific Ocean, Japan and Russia.

'What will we do?' Kenji asked.

'Nothing will stop her going back,' said Maria.

'Peters wants the money.'

'Theodora knows all that. She knew he was dangerous. In with the wrong people. Peters is the opposite of Jack. When he took an interest in Theodora – after Jack's death – she used him. She punished him for thinking he could be as good as Jack.'

Maria leaned back in the high chair and closed her eyes for a long moment.

'What would you do if you had to leave the company?'

Kenji felt the tangle of words, as though he were back at language class in Tokyo.

'My opinion,' he said, 'is unknown.'

He took her hand in the silent shadows of the collapsing company.

'Would we be the same without her?' she asked. 'You and me?'

'She brought us together.'

'*La felicità*,' said Maria.

'I remember,' he said. 'Happiness. It was our toast on the first night in Florence.'

When they woke the great city was starting beyond the gently shifting Venetian blinds. A delivery man rang the front door with cartons of exhibition catalogues in English, Italian and Japanese. Kenji admired the elegant cover from *The Light of Navigation* with the exhibition title in golden script. For the first time he read the introduction Appel had sent separately to the printer. There in the final paragraph he recognised a fragment from the paragraph he gave her for the letter to Maria. These maps are our consolation.

XIX

KENJI WAS TEN BLOCKS from the AT&T Tower when he saw the searchlight swivelling like some Hollywood beacon from long ago. It was Maria's idea. He felt a surge of anticipation as the purposeful beam shone out through the highboy top of the salmon granite skyscraper. The title he chose for the exhibition fluttered on a maroon banner in the loggia. *Where it Was and As it Was.*

The director of Appel's New York gallery was giving a television interview as Kenji entered. Red-jacketed waiters moved swiftly through the exhibition space with trays of champagne and Italian wine. A huge Beauvais tapestry of Chinese astronomers studying a globe was suspended in the soaring hall. A quartet played Vivaldi beside the Marco Polo fountain. Precise jets of water surged from the mouths of turtles and sparkled in the spotlights. Kenji watched the guests read his captions and point to the wind allegories, mermaids and colourful banners of forgotten domains. There was a fifteenth-century etymological volume with the first printed T-O map of the world. A text board explained the reintroduction of Ptolemy's geography to Europe and how old schemes coexisted with new theories. A 1541 Waldseemüller map showed the mythical island of Hy-Brazil off the coast of Ireland. An eighteenth-century time map by Girolamo Martignoni presented the flow of history in the form of rivers and tributaries. The six volumes of Stokes's *Iconography of Manhattan Island*, the most important reference work on New York maps and views, lay open in a walnut display case. Two *Hydrographie Française* atlases lay side by side to mark the bicentenary of the French Revolution. The first was opened at the title page with royal insignia. In the post-Revolution edition the printing plate had been reworked – the King displaced by a revolutionary woman with bright eyes and dangling curls.

To one side Kenji saw a cluster of staff from Rare View. One of them embraced him. They talked excitedly about the celebrities, art correspondents and clients. Someone asked if it were true about the auction estimates. Before Kenji could answer, the brilliant glare of a television spotlight picked out Theodora Appel at the entrance. She wore a black Cannes gown, a fine gold necklace with a single pearl and Jack Berman's watch. Kenji scrutinised her face for some reaction to the demands from Lewis Peters. But she was serene as she moved through the throng, acknowledging guests by name. Kenji was profoundly moved to see her. In a moment of elation he dispelled the notion that anything could possibly be wrong. The whole array seemed to find in her illuminated presence the focus of its magnificence. There was a voice behind him.

'We always seem to meet at these things.'

'Curtis!' said Kenji. 'You came.'

'Just look at all this,' he said, taking in the scene. 'It's even better than your exhibition in Tokyo.'

'Maria organised the best parts.'

'Don't be modest – congratulations!'

'We're going to take it to Japan – to the department store.'

'Get that roof garden going!'

'You have a good memory.'

A waiter approached.

'No refusals this time.'

They raised their glasses.

'To the exhibition,' said Curtis.

'And to Theodora Appel.'

'Kenji, I'm hearing bad things around town – about Theodora – and the company too.'

'Yes, I heard something about that as well.'

He was about to tell Curtis that Appel had bought the palazzo in Florence. But he stopped when the bride and groom from Louisville rushed towards them.

'I wasn't sure we'd be let in!' said the man, grabbing Kenji's hand.

'Without an invitation,' said his wife. 'But the security man spoke to someone and let us in.'

Curtis backed away, silently raising his glass.

'We flew in from Europe last night,' said the groom.

'Our honeymoon,' said the woman. 'We saw the notice about the exhibition in a magazine.'

The man leaned towards Kenji and lowered his voice. 'I'm so glad that misunderstanding with Theodora is over. We just met her and – she was so gracious. This is going to be the beginning of something wonderful. I can tell.'

'I love Theodora,' said the woman. 'It's so sad about Jack.'

Kenji walked through the exhibition as though looking at the maps for the first time. On an engraved chart by Benjamin Franklin the Gulf Stream was shown as a river in the Atlantic. He intended to show this to Captain Bonne, whose charts were on loan near the entrance. He turned, hoping to see the Captain somewhere in the crowd. But it was Theodora Appel.

'Staying out of the spotlight – as usual.'

For the first time he shook her hand.

'Congratulations, Kenji. This is absolutely marvellous.'

'I always wait until the day after,' he said. 'Who knows what they'll say?'

They laughed.

'You've got the balance right,' she said. 'It's perfect.'

'There's not so much about progress,' he said softly.

'Oh, but there is! Now it's right. The past is here on its own terms.'

Kenji took the ceramic flask of Japanese sake from his pocket.

'I brought this from Japan. It's for you. For a day like today.'

'Thank you, Kenji – this is so thoughtful. I'll ask them to send it to Rare View. Just for us.' She took his elbow. 'Come on – our friends are over here.'

Maria, Klara and Palmiro were standing under the wooden dome of the Ionic folly. A copy of the constellation fresco in San Lorenzo was painted in the concave vault resting on eight pillars.

'It's an *apparato effimero*,' said Palmiro. 'That's what we call this in Italy. An ephemeral apparatus. Temporary structures like this were made for the great occasions of church and state – coronations, canonisations, weddings.'

'It is beautiful, Palmiro,' said Appel.

'He used gold leaf for the stars,' said Maria.

'Let's find a home for this after the exhibition,' said Appel.

Maria took Kenji's hand and they went to look at the guest book, quickly filling with uninhibited compliments and exclamation marks. The portrait of Abraham Ortelius – left over from the breaking of the atlas – hung above in a gilded frame.

'It seems your visit to Captain Bonne was a help,' said Maria. 'He's coming to Rare View next week.'

'Is he here tonight?'

'No. He's out of town. He phoned this morning.'

'Can he help us?'

'He'll try. He's very fond of Theodora.'

Klara came over and told Maria the Italian consul general had arrived. Kenji found the Hitachi executives and gave them an introduction to the rarest maps. When he went to the entrance, an unlit cigarette in his hand, he saw Appel in the loggia. She posed for a photograph with the chairman of AT&T, spoke to some of the guests and then stepped out into the light of the giant swivelling beam.

When he woke in his hotel room the next morning Kenji phoned Rare View. Before anyone could answer, he replaced the receiver. He had nothing to say. At the gallery he clipped the review from the newspaper inside the door. He made a sign referring clients to the exhibition – the gallery would be closed for a week. Then he walked over to Central Park and along Fifth Avenue. He had no destination until he came to the Frick Collection. On previous visits he enjoyed the calm of this oasis. But now he felt anxious. He returned to the gallery, picked up the car keys and drove south to the Lincoln Tunnel.

The breeze at Rare View still had the heat of summer – as

though coming from a summer far away. There was a glow from the desk lamp in Appel's office. As Kenji was about to open the front door he heard footsteps from the other side. He reached for the clipping in his pocket so he'd have something to say. When the door swung open he held it up.

'Oh – thank you,' said Appel. 'Come on – I need some air.'

They walked to the back of the house and down through the trees.

'Where's Maria?' she asked.

'In New York. There were a lot of enquiries after the opening.'

'It's best she stay there a while. The first days will be busy. We need it to go smoothly.'

Kenji followed her path through the long grass.

'What will we do?' he asked.

'Your exhibition could turn the market. Buy us time.'

Kenji wanted to tell her about his visa. But he couldn't.

'I've been doing some weeding,' she said. 'I made a fire over there.'

Blackened embers still glowed in the apron of ash. Appel pushed one of the logs with her heel and sparks shot high overhead. She folded her arms as though the embers had given out something cold. Then she looked at him with a quizzical smile. At that instant Kenji thought she was going to say something about himself and Maria. But she said something else.

'Where did we find you, Kenji?'

It was what the staff called an Appel question. Something to disturb the equilibrium – to evoke a response. But this time, it was the question that was revealing – a sort of admission. At first it came as a shock. There had been a flicker of realisation the night before – while reading the comments in the exhibition guest book. Now he had no doubt. It was Curtis Hahn who told the Japanese interpreter to write the complaint that brought him to America.

'You found me at a department store in Tokyo,' said Kenji.

'Yes,' she said, turning back towards the embers. 'At a department store in Tokyo.'

X X

THAT NIGHT HE DREAMT the telephone was ringing. Then it broke into his dream. Kenji went to the living room and answered. There was silence at the end of the line. He lowered the handset to the sideboard. It was a short drive in the late summer night. From the driveway the beams lit up the house and the Momiji tree. When he turned off the engine the delicate foliage disappeared as though Rare View itself had been a stage.

In the office where he had watched her work he caught his frozen reflection in the glass of the framed museum poster. There was almost a tone in the silence of the room as Theodora Appel's body lay between the desk and the window. There was a small pool on the floor. If he could have moved he'd have changed the shape of his mouth – a kind of smile – like a Kabuki smile that can mean many things. There was a clean cavity in the timber of the terrestrial globe. Part of its varnished gesso was shattered into the Atlantic. The telephone receiver was dangling from the desk. He went to the library and called the ambulance from there. The police came first. They asked about the upstairs bedroom he'd never seen. It was strange to hear footsteps up there when she was gone. A window in the main gallery had been smashed and a side door from the garage was splintered. A detective speculated that there were two of them. Kenji called Maria from the library.

'Theodora is dead.'

She hung up without a word. He went outside and sat in the long grass, staring at the swirling lights casting strange colours across the property. A police officer spoke to a dispatcher. She was forty-seven, he said. In his mind Kenji could see her again – the strobe on her gentle Italian tan at the gala opening in New York. He walked away to the treeline. An apron of grey ash between the trees was all that was left of the fire. But it was too early to be burning leaves. She was burning Rare View records, and papers she couldn't take with her.

At the funeral in suburban Philadelphia, Jack Berman's brother sat in the front pew with Klara, Maria, Palmiro and Captain Bonne. Kenji sat behind with Scott who sold the stolen maps back to Appel, Curtis who found Kenji in Tokyo and the two accountants. Phil, who accompanied Kenji to Louisville, sat alone at the back of the church. There were no clients. Theodora Appel was buried with the man she loved. At the Berman house in Bryn Mawr they recalled how they'd first met her, and laughed about the early, chaotic days at Rare View. Klara sat on the sofa between Maria and Kenji.

'Theodora said the exhibition was so beautiful. We know how hard you tried.'

'I still don't believe this,' said Palmiro.

'They've arrested two men,' said Scott. 'One of them used to work for Peters.'

There was a long pause.

'Theodora once told me about a place near here,' said Maria. 'It's called the Blue Route – a section of unfinished interstate. The proposal in blue was chosen over the others. But there's a planning problem. It's been held up for years.'

They drove to Villanova and walked down the embankment to the unfinished stretch of road. A couple of joggers glanced away – knowing these formally dressed people were there to remember or to imagine. They stood at the end of the unfinished interstate looking at the brambles and the wild blossoms moving gently in the breeze. Then they turned and walked back along the empty road.

XXI

DELICATE ORIENTAL IVY GROWS on the facade of the Istituto Italiano in Tokyo. You tell me Nagasaki was the Naples of the Orient. On a wall map you point to Mito, your home town.

'It means "myth".'

'Yes,' I reply. 'In Italian, *mito* is "myth".'

At the Kabuki I'm reminded of our evening at the Delacorte Theater in Central Park. Tonight there's a special ceremony. The company kneels in line as players being elevated pay homage to their mentors. They take new but ancient names. You say it's strange to hear actors use their own words. From a building overlooking the gallery where you once worked, we look out at the green asphalt roof garden. Long ago there were telescopes and a zoo. Together we visit the library at the Jesuit university. Here is a map of Japan by Luis Teixeira, a Portuguese cartographer to the King of Spain. The horizontal islands are coloured in yellow, green and orange watercolour wash. The towns are tipped in brazilwood and the island of Corea is in cuprous verdigris. In another map, Japan lies west to east and part of America is shown with a wolf and prancing deer. East Asia by Martino Martini is outlined in heavy green ink oxidising through the page. At Rare View Theodora told us the green pigments are like embedded timepieces – the copper subtly changing the fine rag paper over time. Now I know she understood time – as the great mapmakers understood time. And across time's topography she tried to connect the markings of happy memory, knowing she would fail.

In Mito they're taking down the scaffolding from the new Art Tower by Arata Isozaki. You tell me how much it progressed while you were in America. After the inauguration we'll take an elevator up through the twisting tetrahedrons and look out at the plum gardens and the lake. At the fish farm you hunker at the edge and stare into the water. A woman in an apron scoops a small carp into a plastic bag. From a cylinder of oxygen taller than herself she inflates the transparent vault over the tiny horizon of water.

In Mito there are no Italian newspapers, so I buy the *Herald Tribune* – Theodora called it the 'Paris Herald'. In Florence, she always began the day with yesterday's paper. For the first time I notice the banner artwork – a nineteenth-century heroine reaching into an old-fashioned industrial future – the clock mysteriously set at twelve minutes past six. The figure looks like the statue of Primavera you found restored by the Arno. I remember the day

I saw your ghostly figure high up in the new gallery. And I remember your obsession with progress.

I became her conscience. The Captain said so. I tried to sabotage her purchase of the apartment by taking photographs of that extraordinary ceiling map. I wanted to send them to the Soprintendente of Florence with a note that the fresco might be in danger. That would have delayed the sale – possibly for half a year. Theodora would have had the money to pay back her debt. But she caught me with the camera. She spent recklessly on the place where she once loved – as though time could be bought like space. Did she intend to live in my country? Or was this another investment? Can a ceiling fresco be taken down and sold? I almost called the Washington workshop to find out. But my doubts were ended that evening in Florence. You were at the edge of the terrace when she told me about the day she saw her art historian for the last time – in a hospital room with white walls and a bare white ceiling.

I remember how you moved barefoot over the hardwood floors at Rare View, turning small pieces of paper in your hands. I understand better your circling the Beltway time and again. At first I thought you were confused. But months after your arrival, Palmiro saw you casually pass the exits – circling the city in the trance of night. Now I know better than to think your disorientation any greater than mine. I've seen your fascination with water rushing over the weirs of the Arno, the ponds at Bellosguardo and the fish pools in Mito. You say all the great gardens of Japan have flowing water.

In this month's *Yale Library Gazette* the book dealer who brought the Vinland map to America gives a memoir of the affair. The controversy continues but we are far away. John Paul Getty Jr and the National Heritage Memorial Fund have paid to keep the Hereford map in its cathedral home. Theodora's favourite painting, Pontormo's Halberdier, is gone to the Getty in Los Angeles. The Library of Congress is trying to buy the only known example of Canon Waldseemüller's great map – the first to name America. The stained-glass maps of the old American Geographical Society are still missing. It is strange how these objects seem as restless as ourselves.

Sparks scatter high as they burn the first leaves of autumn in the Kairaku-en Gardens in Mito. You show me the spot where your professor took the photograph for the cover of his translation of Emily Dickinson's poems. There is a rock fountain that's said to cure the eyes. I remember when the cardboard box with your side-tracked research arrived at Rare View. You took it, unopened, to the clearing and set it on the cold ashes near the tree line. On top of it you set the binding of the broken Ortelius mapbook and the client mailing list other dealers were plotting to find. To one side I found a postcard fragment blown out from the fire Theodora had made. The only legible words were: 'Can't wait for winter!' Together we watched the box catch fire and the leather cover burn evenly around the gold leaf title, *Theatrum Orbis Terrarum*: the Theatre of the World.

The New York exhibition was taken down after two weeks. The company was dissolved by then. We have joined the company of ghosts. Captain Bonne rescued the wooden dome with painted constellations from a West Side yard. I think of the exhibition catalogue as a record of our hope. In the night there is a tremor in the deep map earth. Beside you I wake from the depth charge of my dream. My heart beats faster as I imagine Theodora Appel gazing up at the frescoed world and an unfinished compass rose.

A NOTE ON THE TYPE

In 1924, Monotype based this face on types cut by
Pierre Simon Fournier c. 1742. These types were some
of the most influential designs of the eighteenth century,
being among the earliest of the transitional style of
typeface, and were a stepping stone to the more severe
modern style made popular by Bodoni later in the
century. They had more vertical stress than the old style
types, greater contrast between thick and thin strokes and
little or no bracketing on the serifs.